CROOKS TOUR

CROOKS TOUR

by

JANE SHAW

CONTENTS

CHAPTER ONE

EXCITEMENT AT LAST?

"NOTHING ever happens to me," said Ricky Andersen, putting down the book that she had just finished and sighing gustily.

Her friends, Julie Mitchell and Fay Macdonald, had heard this gloomy grumble so often in the past that they did not even bother to glance up, far less answer. They went on with what they were doing, which was in Julie's case cataloguing a batch of new books for the library, and in Fay's case nothing.

The three girls were in the school library doing a spell of duty as library monitors; but as usual Julie was the only one who was doing any actual work— Ricky's idea of being a library monitor was to read all the books, and Fay's was to ignore the whole thing as far as possible and sit thinking her own thoughts.

Ricky's proper name, which she despised, was Erica; fortunately, however, no one called her by it, not even the mistresses except under extreme provocation. She was tall and long-legged, and her hair, which was done in a very neat pony-tail, was smooth and shining and so fair as to be almost flaxen. According to her friends, she had inherited her fairness and startlingly blue eyes from some remote Viking ancestor along with some very peculiar Viking ideas, like this constant itch for excitement. Ricky rather liked to dream about a remote Viking past and compare it unfavourably with a staid Glasgow present, living with her parents and two small brothers in a flat near the Botanic Gardens and going to a staid Glasgow day-school. Her life, as she would have put it herself, was one long wait for something to happen, one long search for excitement. "Not that I ever find it," she would say disgustedly. "Excitement in Glasgow is pretty well lacking." She did her best to remedy this sad deficiency in her life by reading as many thrillers and adventure stories and accounts of the activities of various crooks as she could lay her hands on, and by making the most of any little drama in her distressingly humdrum existence.

Julie Mitchell, cataloguing away with her usual speed, neatness and efficiency, was small and bouncy, with red curls, a turned-up nose, and rather more freckles than she cared for. She was sometimes called Button, although the reason for that had been forgotten long before, unless it had something to do with her nose. She seldom paid any attention to Ricky's craving for excitement and adventure, or to Fay's remote dreaminess, but went on her way like an efficient little bulldozer.

Fay, the third member of the trio, had a pale, delicate oval face and big dark eyes; a lock of fine hair was always slipping over one eye. She looked frail and sensitive but, according to the others, was about as sensitive as an old boot. Far from wanting excitement and adventure in her life, all she wanted was peace and quiet. The occasional excitements worked up by her friends she ignored as far as possible, and very little upset her, very little surprised her. One day, Ricky vowed, she would startle Fay out of her calm and get her excited about something; but so far that day had not dawned.

Ricky had tipped her chair back against the wall and was dreamily contemplating the ceiling with her feet on the table. "The things that went on in that book!" she said with reminiscent relish. "Kidnapping and murder and international spies and general skulduggery! I'm amazed that Wee Teeny allowed it in the library. Don't you think it's jolly careless of the senior English mistress letting a book like that into the school library? It might give us ideas."

Julie said nothing. She pushed a pile of books across the table to Ricky. "Get on with writing up the cards for these books," she said, "or we'll never be finished before the bell goes. And take your feet off the table in case one of the staff comes in. They're so jolly fussy."

"Bossy old Button," said Ricky, nevertheless doing what Julie told her. "But what about Fay? What's she doing for her living?"

"Nothing. As usual," said Julie.

"I'm thinking," said Fay calmly, putting on the expression that a young and misguided member of staff had once described as *spirituel*, which had made her friends laugh themselves silly. "Surely you know that the thinkers of this world are just as important as bustling old busybodies like Button? If not more so."

"Well, not when it comes to cataloguing books," said Ricky, scribbling cards in her slapdash way until Julie could stand it no longer and took over the cards herself.

So, as they went on with their jobs and their various lessons, nothing more was said about Ricky's taste in literature and her urge for excitement, but it was that very same day, in the French lesson at the beginning of afternoon school, that Miss Elliott, their form-mistress and senior French-mistress, made an important announcement. In the past it had been a school custom to arrange a tour to Paris for girls from the Upper Fourth; this year it had been suggested that the tour should be extended; and she and Miss Miller, who also taught languages, were ready and willing to take a party to Switzerland and Paris for two or three weeks in July. She gave the girls a letter about it to take home to their parents.

"Switzerland and Paris!" said Ricky wistfully, as she and her friends walked down the hill to the bus-stop after school. "Wouldn't that be great! I bet there's plenty of excitement in Switzerland and Paris!"

"D'you think your people would let you go?" Julie asked.

"I shouldn't think so," said Ricky gloomily. "They're always moaning about school fees and bills and that sort of thing. What about you?"

Julie, who had three brothers who also seemed to

cost their parents a good deal, said that she didn't think there was much hope. "Although," she went on, "Mother's mad on us learning languages. If this trip helped our French and German she'd be on to it like a shot—"

Fay said incredulously, "Is this trip to help our *languages*?"

"Yes, didn't you listen to Ellie?"

"Well, of course not. I thought it was for fun. And I didn't think it would be much fun going to Paris with Ellie."

"Och away, of course it would be fun!" cried Ricky. "Ellie couldn't be with every single one of us every minute of the day and night! We'd be bound to have some fun. Besides, she's not a bad old stick. And Dusty Miller is quite merry in an antique sort of way. I'd love to go. Would your people let you, Fay?"

Fay, who was an only child, thought that they might. "But I wouldn't want to, if you two weren't going," she said. "Goodness, I might get landed with that stuck-up Denise Scott! She's sure to go because she had a French grandmother and she's always dying to show off her French. Imagine if I got landed with her!"

"Or Wendy Graham and Mary Pettigrew and that dim lot!" shrieked Julie. "I'd rather stay at home."

I expect I'll have to," said Ricky, reluctantly giving up her dreams of excitement in the high Alps or adventure in some sinister back street in Paris. "I don't think my parents would ever let me go—"

But, as it happened, this time Ricky was doing her parents less than justice. Mr. and Mrs. Andersen, discussing it over dinner that evening, were enthusiastic about the scheme. Mr. Andersen, who was a lawyer, thought that the cost was very reasonable. Mrs. Andersen said that as the trip wouldn't interfere with the family holiday in the Isle of Arran in August, she didn't see why Ricky shouldn't go. It would be better than having her under her feet all July telling her that there was a sinister gang watching the house. Even the little boys, inclined to be jealous, gave in with a good enough grace if Ricky would promise to bring them each back a Swiss army knife. "One with all the gadgets, mind," said David. "Not one of yon miserable wee things with only two blades."

Ricky, ready to promise anything, bolted her apple dumpling, normally one of her favourite puddings and one that she liked to linger over, and flew to the telephone. She rang Fay, the more hopeful, first, and poured a confused jumble of excitement, hopes, fears and sheer rubbish into her ears. "But it won't be any good if you and Button can't go!" she finished. "Oh, if only you could go! Fay, is there the faintest possible *chance*—"

"Och yes," Fay answered calmly when she got a chance. "Daddy says I can go if I want to—"

"Oh *Fay*! Oh how—! Goodness, excitement at last, and you stand there as calm as if you were going for a sail to Dunoon!"

"Well, actually I'm sitting on a wee stool," said Fay.

"But as I haven't finished my dinner I'll go now and have my pud. Why don't you ring up Julie?"

"Oh, I'm going to! Can I say you're definitely going for sure?— Yes, well, you chump, naturally not, but are you *likely* to break your neck before the twenty-seventh of June? Anyway, I'll ring you back—"

"After I've had my pudding," said Fay cautiously. "'Bye."

Fortunately, Julie had finished her pudding, and was prepared to spend an indefinite time on the telephone— or until her father, who was a doctor and who visualized a rapidly diminishing practice because his patients couldn't reach him, pushed her off—listening to Ricky's rhapsodies. For Julie's parents too, especially her mother who luckily had this thing about languages, had thought the tour was a good idea and had almost promised that Julie should also go.

"*Almost* promised?" asked Ricky doubtfully. "Isn't it dead certain?"

"Och well, you know what parents are like," said Julie. "Full of if's and but's and things like good reports. But I think it's pretty certain and I cut out a skirt for Switzerland before supper. I think it's going to be quite nice—"

"It's going to be heaven, heaven, *heaven*—"

"How d'you know, when you haven't even seen the material—"

There was a blank silence at the other end of the line, followed by one of Ricky's shrieks. "Are you talking about your silly old skirt; as if *that* mattered," cried Ricky who at this time of her life wasn't greatly interested in clothes. "I'm talking about the *trip*. I'm so excited I could burst—"

"Well, don't burst yet because my Ma wants to talk to yours—"

"About the trip?"

"Yes."

"Oh, heavens, yes—well, heavens, I'll get her. See you to-morrow. We can talk about it properly then—"

CHAPTER TWO

CROOK IN THE STATION

So, AFTER endless talk and excitement and raised hopes and bitter, though luckily only temporary, disappointments, there they were in a *rapide* being borne through the smiling fields of Champagne on their way to Switzerland. So far the journey had been extremely interesting, but not notable for any very exciting adventures. They had flown to Paris, and Ricky had been sick on the plane which had embarrassed her very much and had prevented her from looking about her for possible smugglers, cut-throats, murderers, international crooks, spies and people like that. As soon as she recovered a little, however, she cast some very suspicious glances at an inoffensive little man in a beret, because it was well-known that the least likely-looking persons were often the most dangerous characters; but, after all, he proved a great disappointment as he was met at the airport by a wife and five children.

Paris had been a confused taxi-drive across the city from the air terminal at Les Invalides to the Gare de l'Est, with occasional awe-inspiring glimpses of such well-known landmarks as the Eiffel Tower and Notre-Dame.

The *rapide* was very smooth, comfortable and clean, not divided up into small compartments like the trains at home, but with long open carriages where you could look round at your fellow-travellers in comfort. Not that they were much to look at, as a great deal of the carriage was taken up with the school tour and all that Ricky had to look at on the other side of the aisle was a rather depressing batch of goody-goodies like Wendy Graham and Mary Pettigrew, Sheila Sutherland and Denise Scott. Wendy, who was an indefatigable photographer, was hung about with camera, tripod, light meter, telephoto lens and various filters. Mary was writing up her diary in a large and not very pretty pad with a spiral top like a reporter's notebook. Denise was practising her French already in a most awful showing-off way. Fortunately the steward who brought their lunch didn't seem to have the faintest idea what she was talking about. Ricky was thankful that they weren't going to the French-speaking part of Switzerland, which would have made Denise unbearable, but to Rosenberg, above Interlaken, in the Bernese Oberland, where they spoke German or what Miss Miller called Schwyzerdütsch which was the Swiss language—Ricky hoped that Denise couldn't speak a word of *that*.

Farther along the aisle was another batch of girls, Alison Fyfe, Margaret Smith and Jean McLeod, nice harmless girls if not particularly interesting; Ellie and Miss Miller were sitting with them, poor things. Ricky, Fay and Julie were very nicely placed, by themselves, and in the next division were sitting Barbara Burnett and Ruth Kerr who were a mad sort of pair, but quite good fun. They kept jumping up and leaning over the top of the partition between the seats to point out some interesting feature of the landscape.

They crossed into Switzerland and at Basle, not far from the frontier, they were to change trains. Julie always came into her own on these occasions and bustled round like a mother hen collecting up her chicks and making sure that no one had forgotten coats, cameras, cases or anything of that kind. Ricky and Fay felt that they could have managed quite well by themselves without all that fussing and bossing; still, if it made old Button happy. Denise was busy talking French to all the porters who were carrying the girls' luggage. This was not very successful for they all pretended that they couldn't understand her. One actually said, "Sorry mees,—No spik English." Ricky and Julie and Fay grinned at Denise who looked rather offended. "You would think that being so near the French border he would understand French," she said. "I suppose he comes from some other part of the country and doesn't understand French."

"He obviously doesn't understand your French," said Fay. "I expect he's French."

The train into which they now all climbed was the old-fashioned sort, but very clean and smart too, with white lace antimacassars on the cushions. Julie installed the girls in a compartment with Ruth and Barbara and they spread themselves out as much as possible and looked unwelcoming when any other travellers passing along the corridor looked in hopefully.

Miss Elliott came in to see that they were all right. "We don't leave Basle for another half-hour," she said. "You can go off and stretch your legs if you like. But be back in twenty minutes and not a second longer. I don't fancy any last-minute panics and people missing the train."

Ricky, Julie and Fay said that of course they wouldn't miss the train and bundled out of the high, foreign train on to the platform immediately. There was a big attractive-looking buffet opposite the platform where the train was standing for which they made a bee-line. Ricky was dying, she told the others, to buy her first bar of Swiss chocolate. They passed an open-air restaurant right there in the station—"A bit different from the Central Station at home in Glasgow," Julie remarked. "The table-cloths would be black in five minutes"—and found themselves in a huge hall. This was a very interesting place, with lots of nice shops and an office for changing money into Swiss francs, besides all the usual things like ticket-offices and left-luggage departments that one expected to find in a station.

The girls walked about very happily, enjoying the foreign sights and smells and Ricky bought her chocolate and they enjoyed that too; and they had almost forgotten about the train—although Julie was just about to remind them—when suddenly a great uproar broke out at the far side of the big hall and a tall fair young man burst into view and came running towards the girls, hotly pursued by two rather stout porters, in blue smocks, who were shouting and waving their arms.

Ricky's bright blue eyes blazed with excitement. "Here's something at last!" she muttered. "He's running away! He's a crook! He must have robbed a bank or something! Look, the wee fat porter is yelling and shaking his fists! They're yelling *Stop thief*!"

"As they seem to be yelling in a foreign language," murmured Fay, calm as ever, "I don't see how you can be sure of that."

"Of course I'm sure! It's as plain as the nose on your face. Oh help, what'll we do? We must do something! We must stop him! What'll we—oh help—should we—should I—oh *help*—"

She took an uncertain step towards the fleeing young man and two very uncertain steps back again as the young man nearly knocked her down as he flashed past. But Julie, who had very little patience with all this shilly-shallying, muttered, "Oh, stop dithering, Ricky," and flung herself straight at the young man's legs.

Fay, who did not really care for this kind of scene at all, pretended not to know these wild friends of hers, and turned and gazed fixedly into a shop window as the uproar raged round her and people came tearing up from all directions. When she sneaked a quick look a second later and saw that Julie and Ricky had collared the young man and were now trying to sit on his head, she glanced round for a back exit so that she could slip quietly away to the train. But after a moment or two, as she watched the struggling mêlée on the ground, she discarded this plan as unfriendly and cautiously approached the girls who now seemed to be getting the worst of things.

"Don't—just—stand there!" panted Julie. "*Help*—"

"I don't honestly feel it's my sort of thing," muttered Fay, but, as the young man struggled free of the girls' clutching arms and attempted to stand up, she obligingly took a swipe at him with her shoulder-bag. He immediately collapsed on the ground again. Fay gazed down at him, feeling pleased and smiling faintly.

By now a great many people had arrived on the scene, porters and station officials and other travellers. People were grabbing the girls and pulling them to their feet and hauling the young man, still a little groggy from Fay's telling blow, to his feet and everybody was standing round the girls in an angry circle yelling at the tops of their voices. As they were all yelling in a foreign language, the girls were not able to take a very active part in the general discussion which seemed to be going on. They were a little worried about letting go of the young man, but the two stout porters who had been originally chasing him now had hold of him—although, Ricky thought, she didn't see why they should be dusting him down, the wicked crook, she and Julie were much more in need of such attentions—still, as the porters seemed to have a good grip of the crook, the girls felt that they could now safely hand over the responsibility of keeping him in safe custody to them. Ricky and Julie stood beaming round, looking rather like a couple of terriers who had tree'd the postman, waiting for the applause. But the applause, Ricky couldn't help feeling, was rather slow in coming. After all, it hadn't been easy, tackling that great brute—you would think there would be a bit of back-slapping and hand-shaking and nice remarks about presence of mind, prompt action, resource—but, even in a foreign language, it was beginning to be all too obvious that if there was any applause going, it wasn't for the girls. Why, one station official was even shaking his fist—not at the crook, mind you, but at *her*! And the young man's expression was positively malevolent or whatever the word was although you couldn't wonder at that when he was no doubt about to be hauled off to gaol at any moment.

Fay looked round at the furious crowd and the smiles fading on the faces of her friends and decided that this would be a good time for her to fade too, when suddenly a most terrible thing happened. Blaring right out over the whole station a voice came over the loudspeaker saying in English, "Ricky, Julie, Fay, come to the train AT ONCE. The train for Interlaken is leaving immediately. Ricky, Julie, Fay, come to the train AT ONCE. Ricky, Julie, Fay, come to the train AT

ONCE. The train for Interlaken is leaving immediately…."

As the girls said afterwards, it was absolutely terrifying to be yelled at like that so that everybody in the whole station could hear, and very embarrassing as well. Blushing hotly, they turned away from the angry crowd and hurried in the direction of their train, which, of course, they had completely forgotten. At the same moment the young man began to run again. Ricky glanced at him anxiously, but honestly, she thought, she couldn't keep *on* catching crooks for those dotty Swiss who didn't seem in the least grateful but just let him get away again.

The girls went panting up to their train where Miss Elliott, who was almost purple with rage, and Miss Miller, obviously in a state of panic, were standing beside some official-looking station master or guard or somebody who was pretty purple too and looking angrily at his watch. Then the girls were bundled on to the train and the tall young man bundled on to the train too and pieces of luggage were handed up through the window over the heads of Ruth and Barbara, which seemed to be quite the usual procedure on Swiss trains. Then the whistle blew and the train moved off and Miss Elliott stood with the girls in the corridor and lectured them for what seemed like hours and told them how kind it was of the guard to hold up the train for them and to broadcast for them over the loud-speaker and if this irresponsible behaviour was a sample of what she had to expect from them on the tour, then they had better go straight home right away and so on and so on and what had they been doing anyway?

The girls really couldn't think of a suitable answer to this, because if they just glanced over their shoulder they could see that awful young man sitting right there in their compartment, looking as though he was only waiting for Miss Elliott to stop before he had a go at them himself. The girls felt—and looked—very hot, embarrassed and uncomfortable, except for Fay, who looked just as cool and calm as usual and who had, in fact, stopped listening to the lecture somewhere about paragraph three. However, they all apologised abjectly and promised that nothing like that would happen again and Miss Elliott forgave them and went off to her own compartment and the girls rather weakly went into theirs and sat down, avoiding the young man's eye.

Barbara and Ruth bombarded them with questions, to which Ricky replied with embarrassed mutters while Julie made signs and faces at them which they totally failed to understand.

"Well," said Barbara flatly at last, "if you'd just stop mopping and mowing at us, Button, and tell us what you were doing—"

"Yes—" the young man burst in wrathfully in English while Ricky and Julie jumped guiltily and Ruth and Barbara looked surprised. "Don't spare *my* feelings. Just tell them what you were doing. Just tell them that you were attacking me. Just tell them that out of the blue a couple of female maniacs, *them*"—and he pointed a savage forefinger at Julie and Ricky— "jumped at me and knocked me down, and when I managed to struggle to my knees a third female maniac, *her*"—and he pointed a savage forefinger at Fay—"struck me over the head with what felt like a sledgehammer and knocked me almost senseless."

The eyes of Barbara and Ruth nearly popped out of their heads. Ricky, Julie and Fay weren't by any means angels in the form but they had never gone in for this sort of thing before as far as they knew. They looked from the girls to the young man and back again with their mouths open.

It had of course, by this time, dawned on Ricky that the young man couldn't be just the escaping crook she had taken him for. But if he wasn't, then why the dickens had he been running through the station like that with two porters chasing him? "Well," she said, goaded, "what were *you* doing?"

The young man stared at her. "What was I doing? What was *I* doing?" he demanded. "I was running for my train. What did you think I was doing?"

Some of the things that Ricky had thought he was doing—robbing a bank, fleeing from justice, et cetera— ran through her mind. She swallowed. "I—I—" she swallowed again. No, really, it was im*poss*ible to explain—.

"She thought you were a crook," said Fay in her calm voice.

Ricky glared at her, and the young man stared. Then

he burst into a bellow of laughter, and soon they were all laughing, which eased the tension considerably, and very soon they were all the best of friends.

"No, but honestly," the young man said eventually, "did I *look* like a crook?"

"Och, you don't need to look like a crook for Ricky to think you are a crook," said Julie. "Ricky's got crooks on the brain."

"Well maybe I have," said Ricky, "but it was you who knocked him down."

"Well, you were standing there dithering and muttering and jumping from foot to foot like a hen on a hot girdle," said Julie. "Somebody had to do something."

The young man laughed again. "That's right," he said. "Knock him down first and work it out afterwards. Much safer."

By this time the girls' nerves had calmed down sufficiently to let them look out at the scenery, which was interesting, but scarcely what they had expected of Switzerland as there was not a mountain to be seen, only ordinary fields and meadows with haystacks in them and very clean, tidy and rather pretty houses scattered about. The young man said that the mountains would come later, and very kindly began to point out the sights to them—the very nice old town of Berne which they passed through, and then at last some mountains, especially a very famous one, all covered with snow, called the Jungfrau; and then on their left a pretty bright blue lake with chalets and villages and an old castle on its banks and little white steamers sailing up and down on its waters. This was the lake of Thun; and at the end of it, they came to Interlaken where the train stopped and they all got out. The school party now had to change trains again; this time they got into a little mountain railway to go up the mountain to Rosenberg, where they were going to stay. The young man said good-bye to them. Ricky and Julie tried once again to apologise for their unjust suspicions and their rough treatment of him but he just grinned.

"Don't give it a thought," he said. "After all, it was thanks to you that I caught my train. Trains aren't held up for people like me, only for important people like you!"

The girls laughed and said good-bye.

CHAPTER THREE

CROOK IN THE HOTEL

THE TRAIN climbed up the valley which became narrower and wilder as they went; huge mountains, snow-capped, rose on either side, towering giants; the girls craned their necks as they looked out of the carriage windows, but even then they could scarcely see the summits. Rosenberg lay near the head of the valley, overlooking at a little jade-green lake, encircled by mountains. It was a fairy-tale village, a huddle of old red roofs climbing up the slope; and the Hotel Alpenblick was the most fairy-tale of all. The house was old and brown and gabled, with gentians and edelweiss carved on the wooden walls, and every window was half-smothered in flowers, geraniums and petunias and little, tight, neat begonias. It was on the edge of the lake, with only a green lawn between it and the water. The hotel-keeper, a jolly little round man, wearing braces embroidered with edelweiss, gave them a tremendous welcome. He talked very fast, inaccurate English, and told them of the many amenities that Rosenberg had to offer—the river and the small lake and mountains, so many, so high mountains, why, look there, face to face with them was the mountain called the Eiger, that terrible north wall of the Eiger which for many years no one had climbed, he had a book of cut-outs from the newspapers telling of the many times that men had not climbed it.

"D'you mean, Herr Diefenbacher, that the Eiger has never been climbed at all?" Julie asked politely.

"Nein, nein," said Herr Diefenbacher, "it had been climbed many times by other routes but never by this terrible north face until only a year or two ago."

Well, honestly, thought Julie, I never heard anything so daft in my life. If it was me, I'd go up the easiest way and have done with it, but she did not say this aloud in case it hurt Herr Diefenbacher's feelings. He was now launched on a pretty full description of Rosenberg's surroundings, the mountains of course, first and foremost, the two glaciers at Grindelwald nearby, a chair-lift from Grindelwald right up into the mountains, Interlaken with its shops of surpassing beauty and its *Kursaal* where many splendid concerts were hearable and where there was a clock made entirely of flowers, and even at that very minute also, a company making a movie-picture down by the lake of Brienz. "And in Rosenberg itself," he said, "such beauty, such flowers in the summer and such winter snow and also very nice shops and more cheap than Interlaken."

Ricky and Fay and Julie had a huge room with three beds in it, and adjoining it was another room for Ruth and Barbara. The walls were of smoothest pine and the beds were covered with snowy counterpanes and great billowing quilts which Miss Miller said were called *duvets*. The windows opened on to tiny balconies and looked across the lake to the towering bulk of the Eiger.

There was a good deal of shouting and laughing and bagging of beds as the girls, calling to each other and running to the windows to exclaim at the view and fighting amiably over the drawers, unpacked. Ricky picked up her case and emptied it on the floor, tossing her things into whatever drawers came handiest; Fay, muttering at intervals that she hoped that they would get some tea soon, she was dying for her tea, quietly took the best drawers and stowed away her belongings with the minimum of fuss. Julie's suitcase was a miracle of neatness, all her things were beautifully packed in little bags, her dresses came out without a crease or a wrinkle. She had everything that she could possibly need—writing-paper, sewing-case, an outfit for cleaning shoes, a little first-aid kit; she even had a tiny clothesline with miniature clothes pegs.

"Come on, come on, let's go and explore," Ricky was calling impatiently.

"Yes, off you go," Miss Elliott said, looking in to see how they were getting on. "No swimming to-day, it's too late, but you can all go and have a good look round. Be back by six to change for dinner."

"No tea?" Fay muttered.

The others ignored this insular demand for tea and they walked up by a little path, bordered with wild flowers, to the village. Small cobbled streets twisted about, full of lovely old chalets and shops filled with tempting bits of nonsense, carvings and embroideries and cuckoo-clocks and musical-boxes, and everywhere the carved bears—sitting, standing, dancing, made into ashtrays, calendars, bottle-corks—which were the symbol of the Bernese Oberland. In some shops they overflowed on to tables on the pavement, and if she had not been restrained by Julie, Ricky would have spent all her money right away on souvenirs and post-cards and presents for her family. They dawdled along the principal street, avoiding Wendy, Mary, Denise and Sheila, those dreary girls, who were window-shopping like themselves, until they came to a nice little open-air café with pink and white striped awnings and tubs of pink geraniums.

"Hah!" said Fay. "Just what I wanted."

The others felt quite disgraced when she ordered tea.

"It makes you look like a tourist," Ricky said disgustedly.

"Well, I am a tourist," said Fay placidly. "Besides, I like tea. I don't like all these foreign foods."

They all gazed with interest at the tea when it came, in a glass, the colour of pale straw, with a little bag floating in it. The others had a fascinating time choosing cold drinks and luscious cakes and dreamily eating them as they gazed out over the valley to the mountains beyond, although the bill, when it came, was not quite so fascinating.

They blamed most of this on Fay's tea.

"We won't allow you to have tea again," Julie said. She, of course, had taken charge of the finances of the trio and was already handing out meager allowances of spending money in a very mean way. "We can't afford these fancy drinks."

The visit to the café did not seem to spoil in any way their appetites for the delicious food that they were given for supper. They had soup, a huge platter of veal, fried potatoes, green beans and a green salad, followed by a creamy, foamy, mountainous chocolate pudding. Everyone had at least three helpings of *that*. After supper they sat outside on the flower-smothered veranda and watched the lights spring up in the houses across the lake and in the chalets far, far up the mountainside, and listened to the faint, sweet tinkle of cowbells. Ricky, who said that Switzerland was jolly nice but it made her simply die of thirst, begged for a drink, so they all had cold drinks. Ricky had ice-cream in hers, but this turned out to be a mistake for it made her thirstier than ever. By this time they were all yawning their heads off and were half-asleep— except Fay, who was properly asleep, sitting bolt upright in her composed way on a hard garden chair— so Miss Elliott chased them all off to bed.

It was fun going to bed with the other four, Ricky thought, like boarding-school. Not that she had the faintest desire to be at boarding-school, but bits of it must be quite fun. Fay was already in bed and asleep, regardless of the chatter and the noise and the giggling. Barbara and Ruth had covered themselves with their *duvets* and were galumphing round the room, pretending to be white elephants; Julie was composedly washing her stockings and petticoat and hanging them on her little clothes-line, which was strung across the room between the window and the wash-basin.

The noise died down eventually; the elephants became *duvets* again and went to bed; Julie hopped into bed and turned out the light. Ricky, whose bed faced the open window, sat up against her pillows; there must have been a moon about somewhere because she could faintly see the steep slopes opposite and the pale glimmer of the lake, and she could see the little, friendly twinkle of the village lights. She hugged her knees and thought happily that here she was, really and truly in Switzerland. She could hardly believe it, it was too wonderful and exciting, she would certainly burst with excitement; she could hardly bear to lie down and sleep, she was so bubbling with excitement. But, of course, if she didn't sleep, the night would take an endless time to pass, and she was dying for the morning when all the adventures could begin. For surely there must be crooks in *Switzerland*? Switzerland, she knew from her reading, was a great haunt of secret-service agents, famous jewel-thieves, spies and the dregs of the underworld in general—surely, she thought, slipping gently down on her pillows, surely she would have the ordinary good luck to fall in with

at least *one* of them? Anv little old dreg would do ...
any quite ordinary little jewel-thief ... she didn't
expect to come in the way of the *head* of an international spy-ring ... just one quite ordinary ...
little crook ... would do....

She did not know how much later it was when she
woke, for she had no watch beside her; outside, all
seemed to be dark and she might have been asleep for
two minutes or two hours. All she knew was that she
was simply dying of thirst. That ice-cream, she
thought, that was a big mistake, I should have had
fresh lemon, like Fay. She lay and tortured herself
for a little, thinking of the lemon, a long tall glass of
it, the outside frosted and the chunks of ice tinkling
against the sides and freezing against her lips as she
sipped.... She swallowed in a strangled sort of
way.... A glass of water, she thought, that would
be better than nothing, a long, long drink of water,
ice-cold from the fridge in the kitchen at home....
She was a long, long way from the fridge in the kitchen
at home, she thought, and she felt suddenly lost and
homesick.... She wondered where the fridge was
in this little hotel? She'd have to do something, she
would be found parched and dead of thirst in the morning if she didn't get up and look for water, but her
courage failed her at the thought of stumbling through
a strange, dark and silent hotel, hunting for the fridge,
why, she would probably fall over a couple of burglars
at least! ... Of course, that had its tempting aspect
too, but perhaps she should leave that sort of thing

till daylight…. But she couldn't leave her thirst until daylight, she wouldn't be alive, she would simply have to find a drink of water some—. She suddenly sat up, giggling to herself. A drink of water! She was a daft scone, there was a *basin* right there in the bedroom! She had only to turn a tap and streams of beautiful, cold, fresh, sparkling water would come gushing out! She flung aside the blankets and jumped out of bed.

Everybody said afterwards that it was her own fault, that she would have been perfectly all right if she had only stopped to think what she was doing for a minute, instead of banging off like an elephant on the charge. But Ricky was never a great one for stopping to think. She darted across the room—and a rope was round her throat and a soft gag was filling her mouth.

She nearly, she said afterwards, died of shock. I mean, she said, I was *dying* to meet a crook, but I never thought that there would be one right there in my *room*, on the very first *night*! She stumbled and fell and lashed out with her arms, but the rope was only round her throat more tightly and the soft gag was filling her mouth and nostrils so that she could hardly breathe.

"Help, oh help," she croaked, but the cry was lost in the folds of the gag. "Help, help—" oh help, she thought, that's no good, that's English! No one in the hotel can speak proper English! Oh what—oh help— She didn't know a word of German, but from somewhere in the dim past, from the depths of her memory, a phrase was dredged up, from a lesson to which she must have been listening by mistake. She tore and clawed at the gag and yelled at the pitch of her lungs, *"Au secours! Au secours!"*

In the adjoining room, Barbara, awakened by the bumps and thumps next door, shook Ruth awake. "Ruth, wake up," she whispered. "Listen!"

Ruth, instantly awake, listened. "Is it one of them walking in her sleep, d'you think?" she whispered.

"Walking?" Barbara whispered back. "Falling flat on her face, more like—"

They listened to the grunts, groans, pants and struggles. "Something going on," whispered Barbara. "Come on—" and at that moment the yell of *"Au secours! Au secours!"* came ringing through the room.

"That's French," said Ruth, surprised. "It means *help*! It must be a burglar or something! Come on—"

They dashed into the next room, saw in the faint light a figure on the floor struggling and thrashing about like Laocoon and the snakes, and hurled themselves upon it.

The din then became deafening and the air rang with such cries as "Got you!" "Take *that*!" "*Au secours*!" "Just you wait … till I bash you!" "Help, Julie, *help*!" and with pantings, gaspings, thumps, bumps and strangled moans, Julie, her sleep rudely disturbed, snapped on the light and jumped out of bed. Miss Elliott, Miss Miller and the anxious faces of Denise, Wendy, Mary, Sheila and the others crowded into the doorway. On the floor lay Ricky, inextricably entangled in Julie's clothes-line, petticoat and stockings, while Ruth and Barbara, sprawled on top of her, thumped and belaboured her energetically.

"But Ricky," said Julie, furiously surveying the wreck of her stockings and petticoat, not to mention the clothes-line, "are you clean daft? You saw me hanging up my wee line!"

"Yes, I know," said Ricky in a small voice. "But I forgot. And it's no joke," she burst out, "having a rope round your neck and a gag in your mouth in the dark in the middle of the night! It's not easy to think with a rope round your neck and a gag in your mouth!"

"And you," said Miss Elliott, turning to Ruth and Barbara, "when Ricky shouted, didn't you recognise her voice?"

"We might have recognized her *voice*. We didn"t recognize her French," said Barbara defensively.

"We didn't know that she knew any French," added Ruth.

"We thought she was a burglar and we just went for her—"

"You can say *that* again," muttered Ricky, tenderly exploring her bruises.

Miss Elliott suddenly began to laugh. "Well, you were pretty brave, even if you *were* very silly," she said. "And I suppose that's something. Now clear up the mess and pop off to bed before you waken the whole hotel—"

"Or before you waken Fay," said Julie, jerking her head towards the bed in the corner where Fay, delicate and ethereal on her pillow, lay sleeping through it all.

CHAPTER FOUR

CROOK IN THE SHOP

SWITZERLAND was wonderful. They swam in the lake and they picnicked by the lake. They went up mountains on funiculars, on cablecars, on ski-lifts, even on foot. They went to Grindelwald and saw two glaciers; they went to Mürren and saw that mountain village up among the high snowy peaks, dizzily perched on a ledge; they went in a steamer from Interlaken to Brienz and saw old wrinkled men carving exquisite cups and figures and little delicate angels out of wood. They ate cream cakes and ices and at least fifty different varieties of chocolate bars. They went to Interlaken, the town between the lakes, and strolled under the lime trees and gazed up at the remote beauty of the Jungfrau. And they shopped and shopped and shopped. Switzerland was wonderful and beautiful—but it wasn't exactly exciting. Not what I call exciting, Ricky thought; no crooks.

That is, until the day the girls went shopping in Interlaken.

Of course they had often been to Interlaken—there was a famous tea-shop there that drew them like a magnet—but Miss Elliott had reserved this day for shopping, as the next day they were going to Schynige Platte, and a tour of three mountain passes, the Susten, Furka and Grimsel, had to be fitted in. Everyone was perfectly willing to spend the day in Interlaken, they could all have spent hours in those little Swiss shops, except possibly Julie, who was inclined to worry about the waste of money. But in any case, Ricky wanted to get those Swiss army knives for her small brothers.

"Well, look," said Fay, waving a vague hand, "the shops are full of them."

"But these are tourist shops," Ricky objected. "These knives are dear enough, I don't want to pay any fancy prices, I want to get them in one of the ordinary shops where the Swiss themselves would buy."

"I expect that the prices are the same wherever you buy them," said Fay, but made no further objection.

So they dawdled along little back streets, and in one little narrow cobbled way, near the river that runs through Interlaken, joining the two lakes, Ricky spied across the road a tiny little watch-maker's that also had knives in the window. But Fay had also spied something, a window full of bells, goat-bells of all sizes, cow-bells from tiny small things no bigger than the palm of her hand to great monsters hanging from leather halters, the very sight of which made her feel tired and sorry for the cows who would wear them.

"*That's* what I'm going to take to my mother," she said, "a wee bell. Ricky is quite right, these are the sort of places where the Swiss would shop, these are real bells for the farmers to buy, not the kind done up for the tourists with pictures of the Jungfrau on them."

They all crowded into the dark little shop. The pretty young girl who served them could not speak English, but it was wonderful what smiling and pointing could do. Julie was rather alarmed at the size of the bells to which Fay was pointing.

"Fay, are you daft?" she whispered. "What's your mother going to do with a muckle great thing like that?"

"Well, I thought a gong," said Fay. "You know that terrible gong we have at home? It came from a heathen temple and I must say it sounds like it. The neighbours are always complaining."

She tentatively tried the note of the bell that she was holding, and, of course, that was the signal for Ricky to try every bell on which she could lay her hands, until the little shop was ringing like a church belfry during a bell-ringers' practice. When Fay finally made her choice and the girls left the shop with the bell wrapped up in a piece of newspaper under Fay's arm, they were all shouting at each other as though they were deaf.

They shouted at the little watchmaker too, which perhaps accounted for the rather hunted expression on his face, although Ricky said afterwards not at all, from the very first she had thought he had a sly look and glanced at them out of the sides of his eyes. However, he had plenty of knives and as Ricky had practised the word *messer*, which was the German for *knife*, with Miss Miller, he produced them right away, without any of the misunderstandings which usually accompanied the girls when they went shopping where the shopkeepers couldn't speak English.

Ricky, who always took ages to make up her mind, was closely examining knife after knife. Fay was leaning up against the counter gently clanging her bell and listening to its note, and Julie was saying in her brisk way, "Now don't stand swithering there all day, Ricky, they're all exactly alike," when suddenly from behind the door at the back of the shop came the sound of a shot.

The girls all jumped and the little man glanced hurriedly over his shoulder. Then there crept into the room the sound of a soft and deadly voice. "Next time," it whispered, "I won't aim wide. *Hand over the papers.*" And another voice, almost sobbing, moaned in reply, "No, no, *no!*"

For a second no one moved; then the shopkeeper, with a strange expression, leant over and banged shut the door at the back of the shop; and Ricky, flinging down the knives that she was fingering, bolted out of the shop.

Fay and Julie found her outside on the pavement, nearly dancing with excitement.

"Did you hear, did you *hear*?" she muttered, as they, looking embarrassed, came out of the shop. "That was the sound of a shot!"

"How can you be sure?" murmured Fay. "Lots of things sound like a shot—a door banging, a car back-firing—"

Ricky said impatiently, "If you think a car could get into that wee shop, you're dafter than I thought you were." And although Fay did mutter that the car didn't have to be actually in the *shop*, Ricky simply did not listen, but rushed on, "And did you hear what the man in the back-room *said*? It gave me the creeps. We'll have to do something."

"What sort of thing?" asked Fay unenthusiastically.

"Oh, I don't know!" said Ricky, beginning to dither as usual. "Go for the police. Yell for help. Get Ellie. Get the —"

"How would it be," asked Fay helpfully, "if I rang my bell?"

Julie said briskly, "Don't be daft. And we don't know where the police are; by the time we got them that poor creature in there would be— No, we'll have to deal with this ourselves."

"D-d-deal with it ourselves?" quavered Ricky.

"Yes. There's obviously some dirty work going on. What would you say, Ricky?"

Ricky tried to pull herself together. "Oh, definitely," she said. "That dreadful whispering creature in there is trying to get those papers from the other poor bloke. I expect he's a secret agent with vitally important papers—"

"He seems to have slipped up somewhere," Fay

murmured. "He's in the enemy's hands now, all right. I wonder what happened to him."

"Yes, well, never mind about that," said Julie. "The things is, we've got to get him away. The shopkeeper is only a wee shilpit creature, two of us could easily overpower him—"

"O-o-overpower him?"

"Yes. Two overpower him and the other one rushes into that room and rescues—"

"But," interrupted Fay, "the man in that room has a gun!"

"Yes I know. And if we don't hurry up we'll be too late."

"Too late!" said Fay in a faint voice.

"Yes, he'll have shot the poor bloke. Now Ricky," Julie went on, "you go in and ask to see the knives again. Fay and I will edge behind the counter. The minute that we grab the shopkeeper, you make a dash for the other room. Be careful that you don't get shot."

Between excitement and terror, Ricky's teeth were chattering so much that she could hardly speak. "H-h-how c-c-can I b-b-be c-c-careful?"

"Well," said Julie impatiently, "one trick I saw on the films is flinging open the door and standing back yourself. Then the bullet from the other chap's gun misses you."

Ricky swallowed.

"Now for goodness sake stop blethering and get on with it," said Julie.

Ricky swallowed again and tried to look brave, then with shrinking steps approached the little shop once more.

The shopkeeper looked alarmed, to say the least of it, at the re-appearance of these strange girls, but obligingly brought out his knives again. Ricky began to finger them; Julie and Fay began to edge their way round behind the counter. There was now only a low murmur of voices from the other room. At least he's not dead yet, thank heaven, Ricky thought, and then hadn't time to think any more for with a wild cry Julie closed in on one side of the little man and Fay, slightly hampered by her bell which she still had under her arm, closed on his other side. Ricky rushed round one end of the counter, but finding that blocked by the swaying mass of struggling figures, rushed round the other end. As she reached the door in the back of the shop, she remembered just in time Julie's advice; she flung wide the door and stood aside.

Nothing happened. No bullet came whizzing past her ear, no enemy hordes rushed out to seize her. Only the arguing, quarrelling voices grew louder, regardless apparently of the hurly-burly going on in the shop. Feeling puzzled, Ricky cautiously peered round the jamb of the door. A small boy with a fair bullet head and wearing a black pinafore was sitting with his ear glued to a wireless set, which was now announcing in dulcet tones that the third episode of the *Mystery of the Secret Papers* would be broadcast at the same time the following Thursday.

Outside in the shop, there was a great deal of thumping, grunting and heavy breathing—and then with a dreadful clangour, someone began ringing Fay's bell. People came rushing in from the street, Fay and Julie were pulled off the little man. He flung the bell to the ground and, trembling with rage and indignation, pointed and accusing finger, at the girls, denouncing them furiously in Swiss.

It was not an easy situation to explain. Fay did not even try. As soon as she heard Rickey's horrified whisper that it was only a wireless set that they had heard, she picked up her bell, flung into a corner by the furious shopkeeper, muffled it with her handkerchief, and began to edge, as unobtrusively as might be, towards the door. Not that she could get very far: the small shop was crowded with people who had rushed to the shopkeeper's rescue and who were now staring at the girls in a very hostile manner.

Ricky and Julie hung their heads and listened to the little man's furious tirade in shame and embarrassment. At the first pause Julie plucked up courage to ask, "Does anyone speak English?"

Whether they did or not, no one was going to admit it, until the small boy in the pinafore, who had come into the shop and was looking at the scene in amazement, suddenly said rather haltingly, "I am speaking a little English."

"Well, then," cried Ricky, nearly weeping with relief, "tell him that it was all a mistake! We're terribly, terribly sorry, but it was all a mistake—"

"Yes," said Julie, "we thought someone was being murdered—"

As the small boy now proceeded to tell his father, the shopkeeper, that these girls thought he was a murderer, the tension did not seem to become any easier. And now on every lip was the word *Polizei* which was quite recognizable in any language. The girls were terrified.

"Look," said Ricky desperately to the boy, "please, *please* tell him that it was the wireless! We heard that thing on the wireless, only we thought that it was in fact real, that all those terrible things were really happening—"

The boy began to grin, then he began to laugh; and whatever he said to the others, they all began to laugh too, until the whole shop was rocking with the hearty laughter of these jolly Swiss people. And as no one seemed to be talking about the police any more, Ricky and Julie too began to smile, although a little doubt-fully, and a little uncertainly. The boy said in his slow English, "My father is not speaking English, so he is not understanding the radio. He is not always liking me to make the noise with it when there are peoples in the shop, but I am wanting very much to learn to speak English, so always I am listening to the B.B.C.—"

Everything was now explained. The rescue party drifted off, still laughing heartily. The little shop-keeper straightened his tie and said something to his son. "My father," translated the boy, "thinks that you are very brave misses to want to fight bad mens!"

Crumbs! Brave! Thought Ricky. That's all he knows! But aloud she only laughed and said, "And now, what about those knives? I'd better hurry up and buy them seeing they led us into so much trouble!"

CHAPTER FIVE

CROOK IN THE MOUNTAINS

THE GIRLS naturally did not tell Miss Elliott about their mad mistake. They decided to buy a box of chocolates or something of the sort for the small boy and present it to him later; meantime they fervently hoped that not one word of this encounter would reach Ellie's ears—or the ears of Wendy Graham and Mary Pettigrew, that nosey pair, either, for that matter.

Next day was the excursion to Schynige Platte.

"Schynige Platte? What's that?" the girls asked. "Is it a mountain?"

"Not exactly, although we go up over five thousand feet to get there. It's a garden, really, of Alpine plants."

This sounded of only limited interest, but Ricky, ever hopeful, supposed that crooks could flourish in an Alpine garden as well as anywhere else. Stealing rare plants, for instance—

"You don't think," murmured Fay, "that you're becoming a wee bit of a bore with this obsession of yours about crooks?"

"Och, I don't think so," said Ricky cheerfully. "I could think of lots of things that would bore you more than crooks if I put my mind to it."

They went in the little train down the valley to

Wilderswil and there changed to another mountain railway, which went steeply up and up, leaving Interlaken spread out below them, towards the mountains above. All at once, as they came out of a tunnel, there was a sudden gasp from everyone in the compartment at the fantastic range of snow mountains that met their gaze, the Eiger, the Mönch and the Jungfrau, those three giants of the Bernese Oberland.

Wendy, anxious as usual to be taking photographs, elbowed everybody away from the window as she tried to get a striking picture. Her friend Mary Pettigrew was scribbling feverishly in her diary. Ricky and her friends were very scornful of this diary. "She's so busy writing in her diary that she scarcely gets a chance to see the things that she's writing about," said Fay, but Mary only said, earnestly, that she had to write down things immediately before she forgot them.

The panorama of the mountains from Schynige Platte was even more magnificent, as peak after shining peak came into view; and in contrast, round the girl's feet as they wandered along the little paths, were hundreds of tiny mountain flowers. Best of all, according to Ricky, there was also an hotel. "The Swiss are good at arranging things," she said, "always a restaurant where you want it." So they all had iced drinks and could enjoy the mountains in comfort.

The Alpenblick had packed a very nice lunch for them—fruit and cold meat and cheese and rolls—and they found a pleasant little grassy hollow where they sat and ate it. When they had finished, and they were all leaning back enjoying the sunshine and the cool, flower-scented mountain air, and listening to the distant sweet music of the cow-bells, someone— probably Julie—suggested that it would be nice to walk down instead of taking the little train. Sheila Sutherland said that she didn't see the point of walking when there was a train there, not like the hills at home in Scotland where you jolly well *had* to walk if you wanted to get anywhere, and they argued this way and that; but in the end Julie, Ricky and Fay decided to walk, and the only snag was that Wendy and Mary also thought that they would like the walk. The trio had not much time for Wendy, who was one of those people who was always right, always pleased with herself and not often pleased with the trio. She had a long face like a sheep with a long nose and a mouth that was all too often pursed disapprovingly at Ricky. Mary agreed with her in most things, especially in her disapproval of Ricky.

Ricky was disappointed. She saw little chance of adventure with that prim pair. "Are you *sure* that you want to walk, Wendy?" she asked, peering gloomily down the mountainside. "It looks an awful long way—"

"Of course I want to walk," said Wendy. "I'm very fond of walking."

"I wish I'd known *that*," Ricky muttered under her breath.

Miss Elliott was telling them to take care, not to get

lost and to stick to the path. Although, she added, the Swiss were good at that sort of thing, even the little paths were sign-posted. Did they remember the different coloured markings on the paths they had seen the other day near Grindelwald?

The girls, not paying much attention, assured her that they would take the greatest care, and the walking party set off.

All went quite amiably, and they enjoyed the views and flowers and the cool shade of the trees as they passed through a wood, until they came to a place where the path divided and which, contrary to Swiss custom, was *not* sign-posted. Julie, who as usual had a map with her, said that they must take the right-hand path, which would lead them straight down to Wilderswil, while the other joined a path that led to some distant mountain or other called the Faulhorn.

Just from contrariness, perhaps, or because she would rather give orders than take them from Julie, Wendy said, "This doesn't look much of a path. I'm sure that the other is better. If it does lead to the Faulhorn as you say, Button, there's probably a fork later on going to Wilderswil—"

"It's not what *I* say," said Julie shortly, "it's what the map says. And there's no fork farther on. I know this path looks a bit faint but—"

"Ellie *said* not to go off the path," said Mary virtuously.

"Who's going off the path?" asked Julie. "This is a path, isn't it?"

"Clearest path that ever I saw," Ricky agreed equably.

"I still think that we should take the better path," Wendy said obstinately.

Julie wanted to hit her over the head, but Fay said diplomatically, "Let's put it to the vote. Who votes we go to the right?" and as she knew they would, the trio voted for the right-hand fork, while Wendy and Mary voted for the other.

"Three to two, *that's* settled," said Julie cheerfully and set off down the right-hand path. Wendy and Mary followed all right, but they muttered rebelliously; and when, after half-an-hour or so, the path petered out and the girls found themselves quite hopelessly lost, Wendy and Mary smiled little smug I-told-you-so smiles. They even wanted to climb all the way up to the fork again, but the others drew the line at *that*.

"We can't go very far wrong if we just keep on going downhill," said Julie. "Once clear of these trees we're bound to see Interlaken and the Lake of Brienz and then we'll know where we are—"

"I doubt it," said Wendy. "I think that we should ask at the first chalet we come to—"

"Okay," said Julie amiably.

But the first chalet that they came to was so hedged about with fences, walls, gates and barbed wire, that they hesitated to go near it, far less knock on the door and ask the way.

"We don't *need* to ask the way," said Julie. "We can see the loch from here. It'll be easy to get to Wilderswil from here. Just follow me and I'll lead you there."

"No thanks," said Wendy. "You led us here as it is."

"There's quite a decent road going off through the trees," said Mary. "We could go that way."

"Well, that would be silly, if you like," said Julie, who had a very good sense of direction, "it's going in the opposite direction, down to Lake Brienz, miles out of our way, whereas if we just go straight down there"—and she pointed—"we're bound to come to Wilderswil. Look, you can see that funny wee airfield that we saw on the way up. We can't go wrong."

"We could come to a deep precipice or a river or something and have to go miles out of our way getting round it," objected Wendy. "I'm going up to the house to ask the way."

They stood in a row under the trees and gazed across the clearing at the chalet. It was new and very pretty, with the usual boxes of flowers at the windows, but at the same time, it had such a shuttered, secret look that they hesitated.

Ricky suddenly said, "I bet it's a hideout. I bet some crook lives here when he's hiding from Interpol. I bet—"

Wendy groaned exaggeratedly. "Spare us your crooks, Ricky, for goodness' sake. Crook's hideout! It's a perfectly ordinary chalet. I'm going in to ask the way."

It was easier said than done; the gate was locked. Wendy rattled and shook and banged it to no avail. "All right," she said, for by this time she was determined to ask the way, "I'll climb the wall—"

Julie said, "Crumbs, Wendy, are you crackers? What's the *point*?"

"They point is that we're lost, thanks to you," said Wendy, "and I want to find the quickest way home. All that I'm going to do is climb over the wall and ask the way. No harm in that, is there? Coming, Mary?"

Mary was not at all keen. It seemed to her that the owners of the chalet weren't exactly welcoming to visitors; if they wanted to keep people out, she didn't think that they would be very pleased if she barged in, but she was used to doing what Wendy told her. "Okay," she said unenthusiastically, and the two girls proceeded to scramble over the wall. The other three climbed up after them and leant their elbows on the top to see what was going on. Which turned out to be plenty.

Wendy and Mary landed rather ungracefully on all fours. They picked themselves up and dusted bits of grass off themselves. Mary was still clutching her diary, and Wendy arranged her camera and other assorted gadgets, which were threatening to strangle her, more comfortably round her shoulders. Suddenly, from nowhere it seemed, a man stood before them. He was tall, with enormous shoulders; he looked exceedingly grim and he had a gun in his hand.

His sudden appearance flustered the two girls, and the gun flustered them a good deal more. Apart from the films, it was the first gun that either of them had ever seen in her life. Wendy went quite white and cautiously began to back away; Mary yelped, dropped her diary and flung her hands up in the air.

With his gun, the young man motioned them to go forward. Mary's foot struck her notebook and she bent down to pick it up. There was an angry growl from their captor and with another terrified yelp, Mary tucked the notebook under her chin and got her hands up in the air again as quickly as possible. For a moment Wendy looked as though she was going to argue, but another furious gesture from the gun soon put a stop to that. She too put up her hands, and at the point of the gun the two girls were marched off through the trees towards the chalet.

Fay, Julie and Ricky dropped off the wall and stared at each other. Ricky and Julie were round-eyed, and even Fay's usual calm was disturbed. She pushed her lock of dark hair out of her eyes and looked at the others with the faintest possible crease on her smooth forehead.

"That was a bit odd, surely?" she said.

"Odd? Odd?" squeaked Ricky. "I should jolly well say it was odd! He had a *gun*!"

"Yes, but why?"

"Why? I *told* you, only none of you would listen to me! I told you! I told you this was a crook's hide-out!"

Julie was looking absolutely flabbergasted. She simply could not believe that Ricky had stumbled on a crook at last, here on a remote mountain in Switzerland—And yet, there was the gun— "It's fantastic," she said. "I never saw anything so queer in my life—"

"It's not so queer," said Ricky, who was by now beginning to get her breath back. "It's just as I told you. This is the hideout of some crook or other, and when Wendy and Mary went bursting over the wall that gunman, who must be one of the crook's body-guards, collared them and marched them off to see his boss. Naturally."

"Oh, naturally," said Fay in a faint voice.

"I can't believe it," said Julie. "I can't believe that you've really stumbled on a crook at last! There *must* be some other explanation—"

"Well, you explain it," said Ricky, her blue eyes sparkling with excitement. "You explain that gun."

Julie couldn't explain the gun. This man, this *thug*, had pointed a gun, a real gun, at Wendy and Mary and marched them off.

"Well then," she said, "if a bunch of crooks has got hold of them, we'll have to rescue them."

"Oh, goodness, yes," said Ricky, beginning to dither, "but how? How are we to rescue them? We can't just go bursting in yelling, 'Unhand these girls.' Shall we reconnoitre or something, first? See if there are other chaps with guns around?"

"No, I don't think so," said Julie. "It'll be too late if we bump into another chap with a gun. We'd better take them by surprise." She thought for a moment and the others looked at her, Fay with resigna-tion and Ricky all eager attention. "We'd better split up," Julie then announced. "One of us can go quite boldly up to the front door as a decoy and the other two can nip round the back and rescue Wendy and Mary. Ricky, you'd better be the decoy."

Ricky lost a little of her eager enthusiasm. "Oh, d'you think so? Don't you think that Fay—"

"Don't you want to be a decoy?" Julie interrupted. "I thought that you were always looking for excitement?"

"Yes, yes I do, yes I am," said Ricky, "I only thought that—"

"Well, here's your chance," said Julie. "Now, what I suggest is this; we get over wall—and make a bit less din about it than those two elephants did—and then Ricky can go off that way—" and she jerked her head, "towards the front door, and Fay and I can keep under cover and creep to the back—"

"*I* thought," Fay interrupted, "I thought I'd sit on the wall and keep *cave*—"

"What good will that do?"

"I don't know if it'll do any *good*, but it'll be more comfortable than crawling through the undergrowth."

Julie looked at her with scorn. "Life can't always be comfortable," she said firmly.

"You can say that again," Fay murmured.

"And Ricky," Julie went on, ignoring these subversive murmurs, "you must keep everybody busy at the front while Fay and I are rescuing those two dim-wits at the back."

Ricky looked pensive. "Keep the crooks and the gunmen busy, you mean?" she asked.

"Yes."

"Oh. How can I do that?"

"Good gracious," said Julie impatiently, "use your imagination. You can think of something, surely?"

Ricky was pretty sure that if there were a lot of crooks and gunmen round her all pointing guns at her she wouldn't be able to think of anything; but after all, she had been dying for years to meet a crook or two and now here was her chance so she might as well enjoy it. So she swallowed that great lump in her throat that always seemed to bother her when she was excited and said as brightly as she could, "Och, sure, I'll think of something," and before her thoughts could dwell too much on what might happen if she didn't think of something, she plunged at the wall and began to clamber over. Fay and Julie climbed up after her.

They dropped into the grass at the other side and rose to their feet. Coming towards them from the shelter of the trees was a tall and very good-looking young man.

Ricky turned and was half-way over the wall again when an arm—extremely muscular for such an elegant young man—shot out and caught her by the ankle. "Oh no you don't," said the man and yanked her down into the grass again.

Ricky stood up—as well as her trembling knees would let her—and stared at him. The funny thing was, that she had the queerest feeling that she had seen him before somewhere—but of course, as she had never met a crook face to face in her life before, that was impossible. "Are you the head of the gang?" she blurted out.

"Oh, so you're English, are you?" asked the young man.

"No, Scottish," said Ricky.

"Worse and worse. You should know better than to come sneaking in where you're not wanted, and you can just get out as quickly as you came in. But not over the wall, thank you, that gets knocked down enough as it is. You can follow me and I'll let you out by the gate. And you needn't think that just because you happened to fall at my feet that you'll get an autograph."

The girls thought that he was raving and became, if possible, even more frightened. For a second Julie had a wild idea of flinging herself on this man—after all, they were three to one—and overpowering him and using him as a hostage to get Wendy and Mary back. But as he didn"t look as if he would be all that easily overpowered, she reluctantly abandoned this scheme.

The man had started to move off towards the gate, with Fay and Ricky, only too glad to get out of this dreadful place, following him, but Julie stood where she was and said, much more bravely than she felt, "We're not going without our friends."

The man glanced back at her over his shoulder and

it flashed through Julie's mind that she had seen him
before somewhere. "Are there more of you?" he said.
"Where are they?"

"Where are they?" Julie repeated indignantly. "If
you're the head of the gang you know quite well where
they are. You had them taken away, you and that
man of yours with the gun!"

A slow and rather impish grin broke over the man's
face. "Andy had his gun, had he?" he said. "He loves
that gun." The girls all glared at him furiously. "He
only got it yesterday."

Ricky was so indignant that, for a moment, she
stopped feeling frightened. "He only got it yesterday!"
she echoed. "Then he's not safe! How dare he wave a
gun around at us when he only got it yesterday!"

"Oh, don't be silly," said the man curtly. "You
don't imagine it's loaded, do you? It's only to keep
people out. It doesn't seem to have worked with you."

"We were in before we saw the gun," said Fay.
"Unfortunately."

"Well," said the man, "I don't care how quickly
you get out."

This was excellent news; obviously this crook didn't
want them in his house any more than they wanted
to be there; but, of course, they couldn't go without
Wendy and Mary. "We're not going without our
friends," said Julie.

"Oh well, come along to the house and get this
nonsense straightened out," the man said impatiently
and strode off, with the girls hurrying after him.

As they went along, almost running to keep up with his long strides, Fay muttered, "Don't you think he's a weird sort of crook?"

"Och, he's just plain daft," whispered Ricky, "but I'll be glad when I get out of here."

"Funny thing is," Fay went on muttering, "I can't help feeling that I've seen him before somewhere—"

"Goodness, I thought so too—"

"I felt the same thing—"

As the leader of the gang and the three girls climbed the little flight of steps to the flower-decked veranda, the man with the gun came out of the house. "Oh, there you are, Andy," said the fair man. "I hear that you bagged a couple of schoolgirls."

"Schoolgirls, nothing," said Andy truculently, "they're reporters all right. Cameras, notebooks, the lot—"

The other man laughed. "Look at them, Andy," he said. "Don't you think that they look like schoolgirls?"

Andy said obstinately, "That other lot yesterday looked like boy scouts, didn't they? And yet they were reporters—"

"Well, go and fetch them out and let's have a look at them."

Ricky's head was beginning to spin. These men had the most extraordinary conversations without a word of sense in them. She tried again. "If you are the head of the gang," she said, "will you make that man of yours let us go—"

The fair man was leaning against the veranda

lighting a cigarette. He snapped off his lighter impatiently. "I wish you wouldn't keep calling me the head of the gang," he said crossly. "Naturally, I'm the 'head of the gang.' I'm Larry Payne, after all."

"Well," Julie burst in, "even if you're the president of the Swiss Republic you can't go about kidnapping—you're *who*?"

The man glanced at the three gaping faces on which consternation and horror were beginning to dawn.

"Not, not—not Larry Payne the film star?" Julie's voice was the merest whisper.

Fortunately, at that exceedingly embarrassing moment, Andy reappeared with Wendy and Mary. Their hair was on end and they were inclined to be tearful.

"*Look* at them," said the famous Mr. Payne. "Look at them, Andy. Do they look like female reporters?"

"Well," said Andy. "Cameras, notebooks—"

Mary squeaked indignantly, "That's my diary—"

Ricky took a deep breath. "Mr. Payne, we're terribly sorry that we were so rude, we had no idea—"

"We only came in to ask the way," Wendy was at her most prim, "and this man pointed a gun at us and—"

A sharp kick on the ankle put an end to this little speech. "Shut up," Fay whispered. "It's Larry Payne!"

Ricky was stumbling on. "Honestly, Mr. Payne, we're terribly sorry but we didn't *know*. There was this man with the gun—"

"And we've been talking rather a lot about crooks lately—"

Andy was looking much more indignant than the famous Mr. Payne. "Are you trying to tell me that you're *not* reporters or autograph-hunters?" he said. "Day and night they try to get in, and it's my job to keep them out. And what a job—"

But Mr. Payne was smiling. "So you really did think that I was the 'head of the gang'?"

"Oh, well," said Ricky blushing, "well—"

"Our landlord *told* us that there was a company making a film in Interlaken the very first day that we came," said Julie. "We should have put two and two together—"

"Didn't you recognise me?"

"Oh, we did, in a way," cried Ricky. "We *all* thought that your face was sort of familiar."

"I don't think I can be as famous as I thought I was," murmured Mr. Payne. "It's very disappointing. And I don't suppose you even *want* my autograph?"

"Oh, yes we *do*, Mr. Payne!" cried Ricky. "Goodness, yes, we *do*—"

Mr. Payne obligingly wrote *Larry Payne* five times in Mary's reporter's notebook.

"And that's the first interesting thing that's got into that blessed diary of Mary's," muttered Ricky as, farewells over and on the right path again, the girls trudged down towards Wilderswil.

"You can say that again," murmured Fay.

CHAPTER SIX

CROOK ON THE GRIMSEL PASS

FOR the next few days, not a word about crooks passed Ricky's lips. She went hot with embarrassment every time that she thought of the famous Larry Payne and the awful things that they had said to him; twenty autographs wouldn't have made up for that excessively unpleasant half-hour. Although, of course, an auto-graph was better than nothing. Wendy seemed to think that it was all Ricky's fault and put on such a prim and disapproving face about the whole thing that Ricky longed to hit her.

"Could *I* help it, if that dotty Andy held you up with a gun?" Ricky asked. "If you had done what I told you and what Button told you, none of us would have put a foot inside that awful chalet."

"Well," said Fay in a dreamy voice, "that would have been a pity too, because Larry Payne was absol-utely fabulous—"

They were sun-bathing on the shores of the lake after their plunge, icy as usual, into its jade-green waters. According to Fay, that lake must have been fed by about ten thousand glaciers, she had never felt anything so cold in her life, not even her own Scottish waters. But, of course, there was a big difference when you came out; in Switzerland you could lie for ages in the hot sun, not like at home where you hurried into your clothes with all possible speed and only a "chittering" bite stopped your teeth from rattling like castanets. On Miss Elliott's instructions, they were having a quiet day, for the next would be their last in Switzerland, and they were going on a tour over three mountain passes, Susten, Furka and Grimsel, to see the Rhône Glacier, to which they were all eagerly looking forward.

In Julie's opinion, they might as well have stayed at Rosenberg and saved their money as it rained for a great deal of the time. But Ricky, impressionable as ever, looked out at the mist and rain, at the wild and desolate scenery and thought that here, in this savage landscape, on these high mountain passes, anything might happen—not crooks, of course, she was finished with crooks, but *something*, and it really was a sell that nothing happened except scenery. That was interesting too, of course, in its way; the Devil's Bridge was terrifying and sometimes the mist parted to reveal jagged mountains and the ever-increasing snow, sometimes there were glimpses of the brave little mountain flowers, gentian or soldanella. As the bus climbed up the Furka Pass the scenery became wilder and bleaker and the snow deeper; beside the road the River Reuss went boiling and tumbling down over the rocks.

The weather cleared when they reached the Rhône

Glacier and they could enjoy the sight of its jagged blue peaks of ice and even walk into the ice-grotto which had been hollowed out in the glacier for the amusement of tourists. It was a startling sight, of the deepest, most wonderful blue.

It began to drizzle again and the school tour hurried back from the glacier to the shelter of the huge shop, full of every conceivable Swiss souvenir, beside the hotel, and they all sent postcards to their families.

"This glacier," said Wendy, who was always handing on information that nobody wanted, "is going backwards."

"What nonsense," said Ricky. "Glaciers don't go backwards, they go forwards, about an inch a year."

"This one is going backwards," said Wendy flatly. "Over four thousand feet in a hundred years. The guide-book says so."

The rain came on again as they went down the valley in a series of dizzy and terrifying hairpin bends, and by the time that they had climbed up to the top of the Grimsel Pass it had changed to snow, and they all bundled into the little inn and crowded round the stove and thankfully consumed bowls of hot soup with their picnic lunches. The tiny *stube* was nice, with white cloths on the tables and bowls of pink peonies and pink roses.

As she ate her lentil soup, Ricky thought to herself how exciting and adventurous it would be if they were all snowed up here for a night or two; she could picture them all warm and cosy round the stove in the lamplight while the storm raged outside. She could picture the door of the inn bursting open to admit— well, who? What kind of a crook, she wondered, could get landed up on the top of the Grimsel Pass on a night of snow and storm? Well, she thought, a jewel thief could, easily. He could have done a terrific robbery down in Andermatt or some such place, there were lots of grand hotels there, certain to be stuffed full of rich ladies with beautiful jewels; and then his car could break down at the top of the Grimsel Pass and he would come into the inn for shelter—

"If you don't *want* jour soup," Fay murmured, "I'll have it—"

Ricky came out of her dream. "Of course I want it," she said indignantly. "I'm starving. Those packed lunches are all very well in their way, jolly nice actually, but they don't fill you up like meat and two veg."

She spooned vigorously at her soup in case anyone else should get the idea that she didn't want it and she also spoke severely to herself. Thinking about crooks again, she must be off her rocker; after that carry-on with Larry Payne she didn't want anything to do with crooks for a long, long time—

The door burst open with a gust of wind and a flurry of snow. A girl came in, shutting the door with difficulty and leaning against it for a moment. She was wearing a white coat and snowflakes clung to her dark hair; she was extremely beautiful.

Ricky, who had a very warm and comfortable seat

near the stove, elbowed her friends out of the way and moved up the bench a little, invitingly, leaving a vacant place. The girl came across the room and sat down with a word of thanks. She held out thin, white hands to the warmth of the stove, and an enormous diamond flashed on her left hand.

The din of twelve chattering girls, which had subsided a little as the stranger came in, rose again. The girl glanced round, then smiled a little at Ricky. "What is it?" she asked, under cover of the noise, in English but with a faint and pretty accent, "a tour of schoolgirls?"

Ricky agreed that it was. "We've been staying at Rosenberg, near Grindelwald," she said, "and we're going on to Paris to-morrow. It's terribly exciting, all this travelling."

The girl smiled again. "You like excitement?" she said.

"You bet," said Ricky. "But I don't get much."

The girl was silent for a moment, then she glanced round and said to Ricky in a low voice, "You like some now, yes?"

"*Yes*," breathed Ricky.

"Then perhaps you will help me," murmured the girl.

"Goodness, yes, anything!" said Ricky, carried away as usual.

The girl glanced at her watch. "You are being here some time?" she said.

"Oh yes," said Ricky, "until two o'clock. Perhaps

you don't know, but there's still such a lot of snow up here that the pass isn't properly open; there's only room for one line of traffic—the cars stop coming up at a certain time and then the cars from this side can go down. Our driver was telling us. We can't leave until two o'clock."

"Yes, I know. That is why I am stopped here. But that perhaps, is all right. He must be here by then," said the girl incomprehensibly. "Then you do this for me?"

Ricky, who thought that the girl was absolutely beautiful and glamorous and who would by this time have stood on her head for her, nodded vigorously.

"Then lend me please, for a small time your striped coat—"

"My blazer, do you mean?" asked Ricky in amazement, glancing down at her blue and green school blazer.

"Yes," said the girl. "I am wanting to hide from someone who follows me. This would be a fine disguise, no, if I am in a schoolgirl's striped coat?"

Ricky's heart began to beat fast with excitement. There was something going on then, at last! This glorious, beautiful girl was in danger of her life! She was running away from some horrible crook or other! Here really was something at last! *This* she wasn't making up, as she had made up all that nonsense about the man in the station and Larry Payne's mountain retreat. This girl was actually in some terrible danger and was asking Ricky to help her! She wasn't making that up. The girl wanted to disguise herself; you didn't do that unless you were in great danger. Her blazer—she giggled. "Goodness, yes, it would be a jolly good disguise—" she was taking off her blazer as she spoke and pulling a scarf out of her pocket "—and here's a scarf; if you tie that over your head and sit among us with your back to the door, he'll *never* recognise you!"

The girl nodded, took off her white coat and put on Ricky's blazer and scarf. "I am like a schoolgirl now?" she asked, her brown eyes dancing.

"Och well," said Ricky, looking at her critically, "not exactly! You've got on a wee bit too much lipstick, for one thing! But that won't matter if you turn your back. Would you," she added, "like me to put on your coat?"

"No, no!" said the girl. "He knows my coat. That I put under the seat—"

She stowed the white coat under the seat but left lying unnoticed on the table her scarf, a gay splash of red and white.

Julie and Fay, who had been watching all this whispering and exchange of clothing with some surprise, could stand it no longer. Julie leant over to Ricky. "What's going on?" she whispered.

Ricky frowned at her. "Tell you later," she whispered back. "Terribly exciting. Being pursued by a crook—"

"Michty me," murmured Fay, "not more crooks."

"Yes, but real this time!" whispered Ricky. "Change

seats with her so that her back is to the door. What's
Ellie doing? Has she got her eagle eye on us? And
Dusty?"

Fay looked across the small inn room and shook her
head. "They're both writing postcards like crazy.
Haven't noticed a thing. Wendy of course, thinks
you're off your rocker as usual."

Ricky cared nothing for Wendy's disapproving
looks and prim mouth. She and the girl changed
places with Fay and Julie. Ricky said, "This is Fay
and this is Julie, they're both going to help you
too."

The girl smiled with great sweetness at them and
said, "How good you are. Thank you."

Julie, always practical, suddenly said, "How did you
get here?"

"Get here?" said the girl. "I am come in my car,
naturally."

"Well, where is it? If he sees that, you've had
it—"

"No, no," said the girl, "that he cannot see. The
car I have hidden behind the inn."

"And what do you plan to do? We have to go at
two o'clock."

"Oh," said Ricky eagerly, "couldn't you come with
us? We could easily hide you in the wee bus!"

Julie thought to herself that Ellie and Dusty would
need to be a lot blinder than they had ever proved
before, if they didn't notice the addition of this tall
and elegant stranger to the school bus; but the girl

was shaking her head and smiling a little. "Thank you, no," she said. "When he finds I am not here, he will go on down the pass to Meiringen and I shall go back to Andermatt and then to Lucerne, where is my home. I—"

She stopped suddenly and her eyes widened and she turned towards the door; the girls listened too, as the high-pitched whine of a powerful engine could be heard approaching.

"There he is!" said the girl in a terrified whisper. "That is his car!"

"Well," said Julie, "don't sit staring at the door or he'll spot you at once. Just be talking and laughing naturally with us like a girl—"

"Of course, of course," said the girl and she hurriedly turned round and bent her head.

Ricky gave a high-pitched unnatural giggle from sheer nerves. Julie glared at her. "Sorry," said Ricky. "I'm just a wee bit nervous, that's all." She fidgeted idly with the scarf lying on the table and kept her eyes on the door. Come what may, she was determined to get a good view of this crook. At the rate she was going she might never see another.

Outside, the car roared up to the door, and even above the noise of the girls chattering and the inter-mittent howling of the wind, could be heard the sound of furious voices. The strange girl kept her head bent. "He is arguing with the landlord," she whispered. "But the landlord will not tell, I am sure. I paid him plenty."

The door was flung open and Ricky jumped about two inches off her seat as a tall man strode in. Goodness, thought Ricky, staring, who would ever think he was a crook? He's fabulous. Much better than Larry Payne—She went on staring at him with her mouth slightly open.

The other girls had all stopped talking to stare too, more or less openly, at this new and extraordinarily handsome arrival; only the little group round the stove showed no interest, but sat still, with bent heads, pretending to talk. The tall man stood glaring round the room at the girls in blue and green and suddenly his gaze fixed on Ricky. He came striding across to her almost sweeping girls from his path as he came. He stood towering before Ricky, white-faced and angry.

"Have you seen a young girl here? Five, ten, minutes ago?" he demanded, speaking English well, but with a strong foreign accent. "She is tall and her hair is dark and she wears a white coat."

Ricky, face to face with her crook at last, swallowed, took a deep breath and stammered.

"N-n-n-no—I mean y-y-y-es. A white coat, I mean a girl in a wh-wh-white coat was here. But she's gone," she finished in a triumphant rush.

"Gone?" he frowned more terribly than before. "Gone? Where is she gone?"

Ricky was terrified. She had never imagined that the creature would *speak* to her. She swallowed again. "She is gone, I mean she went on down to— She *was* here, but she went on down to Meiringen, yes," she nodded, better pleased with the way the conversation was going, "that's where she went, down to Meiringen."

"That is not possible," snapped the man. "No cars are going down to Meiringen until two o'clock."

Oh, blow and bother, neither they are! thought Ricky. Oh, *help*! "Well," she said desperately, "I don't know where she went. But she's not here. You can see she's not here—" and she waved a vague hand round at the green and blue blazers who were all now drinking in this scene with their mouths open, except for the silent one sitting behind Ricky with her head bent.

"Then why," said the man, suddenly shooting out a hand and pointing at the scarf which Ricky was desperately twisting in nervous hands, "then why is her scarf there?"

Ricky gasped and glanced down at her hands. She thrust the scarf behind her back and looked up at this terrible man again. "That's—that's my scarf," she said. She was not at all good at telling lies.

"That's a lie," said the man through shut teeth. "Where is she? If you have hurt one hair of her head I will kill you—"

Ricky blinked and nearly fell off the bench.

Miss Elliott, roused from her postcard writing by the strange scenes which seemed to be going on around her, got up and came across the room.

But, strangest of all, the dark girl jumped up from her seat by the stove, turned to the man and seized him by the arm. "Karl!" she cried. "Karl!" and she broke into German.

The man put his hands on her shoulders, bent down as if he were going to—honestly, thought Ricky, as if he were going to *kiss* her, then glanced round with a grin and gave her a little shake instead.

The girl, blushing and smiling, turned to Ricky. Ricky was bewildered. "Is this, is this not the crook whom you were hiding from?" she asked.

"*Crook*, what is *crook*?"

"Crook? Crook means criminal, the man whom you were running away from?"

The girl, blushing more deeply, laughed. "No, no, I am not running away from a cr-r-r-rook, I am running from this person"—she glanced up at him—"my fiancé. We are having a most terrible quarrel and I would not stay. I say I will never see him again and I run away. But now you hear, you hear him say he will kill you if I am at all hurt. So I think he likes me still and I will marry him after all—" She was taking off the blue and green blazer as she spoke and fishing her white coat out from under the seat. She took Ricky's hand. "Thank you! Thank you ten thousand times," she said. "You have saved me! You shall come to my wedding!" And tucking her hand under the tall man's arm, she went out with him. The girls heard the roar of the high-powered car.

Then everybody immediately began to speak at once.

"Well!" said Ricky, sitting down with a thump. "One big sell after another."

"You and your crooks," began Julie in a scolding voice. "You've got crooks on the brain."

"Ricky, what have you been up to?" demanded Miss Elliott.

The inn door opened and the driver of their little bus put his head round the door. "Now it is time to go," he said.

The descent from the pass was most interesting; they went through deep snow that towered above the bus and under wooden guards built to protect the road from the frequent avalanches. It was even exciting, in a way, for they met a car coming up, against the rules, and it had to back for quite a long distance until it was able to tuck itself into a siding and let the bus pass. But even all that failed to cheer Ricky.

"Och, well," she said, "you can't blame me this time. How was I to know that she was running away from her boy-friend? When she said that she was running away from a man, naturally I assumed he was a bad man. You don't run away from your *fiancé*. Not unless you're daft. All that carry-on for nothing."

Fay took a much more romantic view of the affair. "It was as good as the pictures," she said. "Better, really, because that man was much nicer looking than any film star I've ever seen, even Larry Payne."

"And you must admit," said Julie, "that it was exciting while it lasted. At one point I thought he was going to strangle old Ricky with his bare hands!"

CHAPTER SEVEN

ON TO PARIS

So RICKY came to the reluctant conclusion that Switzerland was no better for crooks than boring old Glasgow, and that it was highly unlikely that Paris would be any improvement on Switzerland. "Och, crooks," she said, "I'm finished with crooks. I'm just going to enjoy my holiday."

It was heart-breaking, said Fay, to leave the Hotel Alpenblick and the little lake and all the lovely mountains; Paris was the only consolation and she only hoped that it wasn't going to be ruined by Denise who had started to roll her *r*'s already.

They had to make three changes on the journey, at Berne, Beil and Basle. This gave Miss Miller great scope for panic as she saw no hope of the party making any of the connections in time. Basle, as a matter of fact, was awful, and the school very nearly did miss their connection. They streamed along by an underground way, dragging hand-cases and paper bags full of souvenirs which they couldn't fit into their luggage, followed by three perspiring porters, while Miss Elliott and Miss Miller, who had the tickets, kept the very cross guard at bay until the girls had clambered on to the train and the porters had pushed the luggage through the windows.

The rest of the journey passed uneventfully and they reached Paris in the early evening. Their first ride through the Paris streets was exceedingly alarming, as the traffic went terrifyingly fast and, of course, on the wrong side of the road. Even Denise, who, much to their annoyance, was sharing a taxi with Fay, Julie and Ricky, was too unnerved to show off her superior knowledge of Paris landmarks properly.

"Yes, well, that's the Louvre—oh help, they're going to *hit* us—there's the Seine—"

"Of course it's the Seine," said Julie crossly, terror making her short-tempered, "we don't need you to tell us that's the Seine."

"Well," said Denise, rather huffily, "I bet you don't know that there are twenty-two bridges over the Seine in the central part of Paris and I bet that you don't know that the Pont Neuf which is French for *new bridge* is the oldest bridge in Paris—"

"People who tell you things like that," said Fay, resolutely turning her eyes away from the frenzied traffic, "are frightfully irritating because they know that you can't check up. You might be telling us the most awful rubbish."

"Well, I'm not," said Denise, "I'm telling you—"

"What's this big square?" Ricky interrupted. "It's lovely! All those fountains and statues and—oh help, did you see that Citröen, it nearly climbed right over our bonnet! It cut right in front, it—"

"This is the Place de la Concorde," said Denise. "Look up there, that's the Champs Elysées, leading up to the Arc de Triomphe—" the rest of her sentence was drowned as the taxi hurtled violently round the Place de la Concorde and she was thrown into Fay's lap.

The taxi turned towards the Place Vendôme and then into the comparative quiet of the little narrow street where their hotel was situated. It was a nice little hotel, with a very ancient and quavering lift, very noisy and rackety, but certainly, as Fay said, a nice relief after that taxi. The girls were lucky with their room again—it was on the top floor, with three beds in it; the room shared by Barbara and Ruth led off it on one side and a bathroom on the other. It was at the back of the hotel and looked over a nice higgledy-piggledy jumble of roofs into a sort of well, round which the hotel was built. Ricky leant her elbows on the sill and looked out. "Goodness, it's nice," she said, "you can see right into all those rooms when the lights are on, it's fascinating. And then if you just look up you can see the stars and all the roofs, *les toits de Paris*," she said suddenly, carried away.

Fay said disgustedly, "If you're going to talk French, like Denise, you can go and share a room with somebody else. We'll have had enough French before we're finished. D'you realise that all the people in the shops and the buses and so on will be talking French all the time, can you imagine?"

Julie, who had unpacked by this time and put everything tidily away in her drawers, came and joined Ricky at the window. "'Hm, very romantic," she agreed, "even the smell is different, but what I want to know is, what about dinner, I'm starving—"

Miss Miller came in then, fortunately, and ordered quick baths and a change into cool dresses. Everybody, she was sure, was dying for something to eat.

When they had bathed and changed, the girls inspected the others' rooms on the floor below. They were very grand and big, decorated in old-fashioned wallpaper and faded gilt with enormously high ceilings and long windows draped in net, but they looked out to the front and had only a view of the narrow street and the long high windows of the houses opposite, not a patch on their little attic rooms, Ricky muttered to the others.

"I'll be more interested in the rooms when I've had some dinner," Fay muttered back.

There was no restaurant in their little hotel—"What about breakfast?" Fay muttered again anxiously—so Miss Elliott led them off to a little restaurant that she knew of; they went along the Rue St. Honoré, which was parallel to the street where their hotel was, and then Miss Elliott dived under a sort of archway and across a tiny courtyard and led them into a jolly little restaurant with red and white checked tablecloths. The school pretty well filled the small place; the owner and his wife smiled and beamed at them, and in no time everyone was busily eating the most delicious food. They would have been eating it in even less than no time if Denise had not insisted on telling everybody what the various items on the menu were and ordering everything in French.

Next morning Fay was, for once, awake unusually early. She lost no time in wakening Ricky and Julie. Ricky got up immediately and darted to the window and leant her elbows on the sill and gazed at their view in daylight. It naturally did not look quite so romantic and mysterious without the lights and the stars, but it was still jolly interesting and Ricky could see into some of the rooms quite easily, and on some window-sills there were pots of geraniums and even, hanging at one, a canary who was singing as if his life depended on it. She was just working out which windows belonged to the hotel and which, such as the ones with geraniums and canary, did not, when she realised that Fay was grumbling away in the background in a manner quite unlike her usual self.

"Well," Fay was saying in a thoroughly anxious, not to say peevish voice, "I suppose Ellie knows what she's doing, but honestly, can we be sure of that? I wondered about it last night, only I forgot to ask her, and now here it's morning and what are we going to do?"

As it was extremely unlike Fay to get into such a state about anything, Ricky left her contemplation of the scenery and looked across at the other two inquiringly.

"What's the matter with Fay, Button?" she asked.

"Och, nothing," said Julie. "She's worrying about her breakfast."

"Why should she worry about her breakfast?"

"If you didn't get any breakfast," said Fay, "wouldn't you worry too?"

"I'd worry all right," said Ricky. "But why shouldn't we get any breakfast?"

"There's no restaurant in this hotel, remember," said Fay, her voice getting anxious again. "I know that French people eat this thing called a Continental breakfast like we had at Rosenberg which isn't like a real breakfast at all, but I must say it would be better than nothing."

Julie said comfortably, "I expect we go out for breakfast and have it at one of those cafe's on the pavement in the sun."

Fay was not impressed by this suggestion. "Well I think it's very eccentric to go out and sit in a café before you've had your breakfast," she said.

Hearing the sound of voices, Barbara and Ruth now came through from their room to join the discussion. They were entirely on Fay's side and were quite prepared to go off there and then to forage for some breakfast in their pyjamas.

At this point there was a knock on the door and in came a pretty young chambermaid staggering under a huge tray. She bade the girls good-morning cheerfully and put the tray down on a table and pushed it over to the window.

"Well I must say," said Fay when the maid had gone, "that's a relief. What do we get?"

They got coffee or chocolate in huge, wide cups, sugar in big flat oblong pieces, a plate of *croissants* and fresh rolls, the most delicious butter, and little dishes of jam. After they had eaten everything, Fay said, "Well, that wasn't bad. Only," she said, "I could have eaten all that *and* some eggs and sausages and things."

After they had had breakfast and had bathed and put on cool cotton frocks—for already they could feel that the sun was hot—they went down in the rickety lift to the hall where there were one or two tables and chairs and where the whole party soon assembled. Miss Elliott, it transpired, believed in letting the girls go about a little by themselves. "My idea isn't to go trudging round all the sights until we're all worn out and everything is just a jumble in our heads," she said. "Notre-Dame you must see and the Louvre and perhaps Versailles, but otherwise I think Paris is much more fun if you just wander and get the feel of the place— see the shops and the funny old book-stalls along the quays by the river and go up to Montmartre and sit in a pavement café when you get tired and watch the people—"

The girls—except for earnest souls like Wendy and Mary who muttered rather disapprovingly under their breaths—were only too ready to fall in with such plans; museums and such-like were all right in their place but very tiring on the feet, and to be allowed some time to wander where they liked—as long as at least three of them went together—struck them as splendid organisation. Miss Elliott spread a map of Paris on the table. "We're here," she said, pointing, "here's the Rue du Mont Thabor; parallel to that is the Rue St. Honoré where we were last night. Here, parallel again, is the Rue de Rivoli, it's full of lovely wee shops, you'll like those. Then opposite are the Tuileries Gardens; if you walk straight across you'll come to the Seine, and if you walk to the left you'll come to the Louvre. Miss Miller and I thought that you could all have a wander this morning on your own, and this afternoon we could go to the Louvre, or the other way about, or if there's some special place that you'd like to see, we'll take you—"

Everybody agreed to go to the Louvre in the afternoon and have the morning to themselves except Wendy, who had been mugging it all up in a guide-book and who wanted to see some boring old museum or other called the Musée de Cluny. Miss Elliott very agreeably said that she would take her, and also Mary and Sheila Sutherland who had been told by Wendy that they would like to go too. Miss Miller said that she was going to look at some pictures and Barbara and Ruth, under the sadly mistaken impression that she meant moving pictures, decided to go with her. Denise, therefore, was obliged to tag along with Ricky and Julie and Fay.

"Och, it doesn't matter," said Julie, as they went up to their rooms to get ready. "Denise isn't a bad old stick. Not like boring old Wendy—"

"It might be jolly useful, having someone with us who can speak French," said Fay. "I mean real French, not the kind we learn at school—"

Well, it *was* useful, in a way.

First of all they walked along the Rue St. Honoré. Denise, for some unaccountable reason, wanted to go farther, to the Faubourg St. Honoré, to have a look at the British Embassy, but the others drew the line at that. In ten days or so, they would be having all the Britain that they wanted and a lot more, they certainly were not going to waste any time on it now. There were very rich-looking little shops in the Rue St. Honoré, antique shops and a heavenly one full of nice things for dogs. Before Julie could stop her, Fay had gone in and bought a drinking-bowl for her dog Mitzi at home. It had "Love Me Love My Dog" on it, only in French. There were nice picture-shops too. One had a very jolly picture of the church in Montmartre which they now knew to be the Sacré Coeur, with snow on the ground.

"Just the thing for my mother," said Ricky, "she adores snow. It's quite wee, it can't cost much. I'll just pop in and ask—"

Julie was always game for anything, Denise wanted to show off her French, Fay did not like going into shops and asking prices, just as she did not like asking people the way, but she did not mind Ricky doing it, so they all trailed into the shop after Ricky.

The little shop was so opulent, with thick pale-grey carpets and an air of quiet elegance, that even Ricky hesitated; but a little dark, plump man, the owner or manager or whatever he was, came forward with such a welcoming smile that the girls all smiled back.

In her best French, which was not, as a matter of fact, all that good, Ricky asked the price of the little picture. The little man named a sum which, even when translated from francs into pounds, was astronomical.

"I don't mean for the whole *shop*, I just mean the price of that one wee picture," said Ricky, startled into English.

The little man laughed. "But yes, I am not making a joke," he said, "that is the price of that one small picture. It is, you understand, an original by Utrillo. You have heard of Utrillo?"

They had all heard of Utrillo—he had come into their Appreciation of Art classes last term. Even so, it seemed an awful lot of money.

"You like the picture?" the little man was saying. "I will show it to you," and he very kindly took the picture out of the window and put it on an easel and let the girls gaze at it with awe. "Now you can say," he said, "when you see copies of that picture, what you call reproductions, in books or in post cards, now you can say, ' Ah, but *I* have seen the original of that picture—'"

He was such a nice man, that Ricky would have liked to ask if he hadn't anything cheaper, but even she realised that if he had, it would still be a long, long way from the ten shillings or so that she had to spend on her mother's present. So they all thanked the little man like anything, and filed out of the shop again, amid a chorus of *au revoirs* and *merci mesdemoiselles* from the little man.

"French people in shops are awfully polite," said Fay. "They say *thank you* even if you don't buy anything."

They now crossed the Place Vendôme, which had a very tall column in it, into the Rue Castiglione and then into the Rue de Rivoli. They loved the shops under the arcades, in the Rue de Rivoli; they were stuffed full of bits of nonsense, gloves and bags and embroidered handkerchiefs and souvenirs of Paris in all shapes and forms. They went into one or two shops, and in spite of Denise's superior French, everybody immediately replied to them in English, much to her annoyance. Fay bought a handkerchief with strawberries embroidered on it.

"You're wasting your money," said Julie severely. "You can't even blow your nose on it."

They then managed to cross the street safely, which they thought was a considerable triumph, and wandered through the Tuileries Gardens for a little. They crossed the Seine by one of the twenty-two bridges and strolled along the river for a while, looking at the barges slowly passing along, or the little white boats crowded with sightseers, and watched the quiet men in berets, sitting on little stools, who were fishing, actually fishing, right there in the middle of Paris.

"Goodness, I like Paris," said Ricky as they wandered. "There are even shops along the quays."

"They're not proper shops," said Julie, "only sort of boxes—"

"Rather like school desks without legs," said Fay, "only, of course, more interesting—"

The boxes, some of which were closed and padlocked, but most of which had their lids temptingly open, were full of books and pictures—prints of flowers or birds, or scenes of Paris, old fashion-plates or engravings. Ricky and Fay and Julie began to rummage, turning over prints and examining the books, most of which were practically incomprehensible, being in French.

"Goodness, I like these boxes," said Ricky. "We might find a priceless treasure in among the rubbish."

"I doubt it," said Denise. "Not nowadays. These are the famous bookstalls of Paris, everybody knows about them. Maybe long ago people could find a bargain here, a rare book or something like that, but not now. Dealers and collectors get there first."

"Oh, I don't know," said Ricky, "something valuable might slip through by mistake."

Anyway, as they wandered from box to box, she kept turning over the prints hopefully, and Julie, the realist, was just about to point out that she didn't know how Ricky was going to recognise anything valuable even if she did come across it, when Ricky gave an excited little squeak. The others gathered round and looked at the print that Ricky was holding up.

"Don't tell me you've actually found a treasure!" exclaimed Julie, amazed.

"Treasure?" said Ricky absently. "Oh, I shouldn't think so. But isn't it rather sweet? Look, it's a little square, called the Place du something or other, Tertre or something like that, it's not very well written—and it's snowing. It really is sweet, I'd like to buy it for my mother. Denise, you ask how much it is—"

Denise obligingly asked the ancient old lady dressed in rusty black, who was in charge of the bookstall, the price of the little picture, and Ricky was very agreeably surprised when it turned out to be only a few shillings.

"Goodness," she said, "that's more like it, not like all those thousands of pounds for that Utrillo. I can manage five shillings—"

So the old lady kindly rolled it up in paper for her and said *merci mademoiselle* and *au revoir, mesdemoiselles,* a great many times in the polite way of the French shopkeepers, and the girls strolled on. They strolled right along the Boulevard St. Michel, or the Boul' Mich' as Denise airily called it, right to some pleasant gardens where they sat down on the rim of a large fountain and gazed at the children playing round them and at an imposing palace in the distance.

"Where are we?" asked Ricky. "What's that building?" Denise did not know, but Julie, studying her map, said, "Well, if that was the Boulevard St. Michel or Boul' Mich' as Denise calls it, that we walked along, then this must be the Luxembourg Gardens and we're a jolly long way from the hotel and we had better be getting back—"

"Couldn't we take a bus or this thing they call the Métro?" said Fay. "I'm worn out—"

The others looked slightly alarmed at this bold suggestion. Nobody felt at all capable of catching the right bus, asking for the tickets and getting off at the right place. As for this thing called the Métro, the Glasgow subway, they felt, was no preparation for the intricacies of the Paris Métro.

Julie said doubtfully, "Would *you* know what bus to take, Denise?"

Denise shook her head. "When I was here before," she said, "we went everywhere in taxis."

"*That's* a brilliant idea," said Fay, whose feet were sore with all that strolling. "A taxi is foolproof. You just tell the man where you want to go and he takes you there—"

Julie began to mutter about the expense, but the others told her not to be an old meanie and they hurried out of the gardens and stood by the side of the road, looking hopeful. A taxi drew up in no time, rather a ramshackle affair with a very ancient driver, and they all piled in. "You tell him where to go, Denise," said Julie.

"And don't give him the story of your life beginning with your French grandmother," said Ricky, "like you usually do. Just tell him where to go—"

Denise looked slightly offended and began to talk to the driver. He seemed to have a certain amount of

difficulty in understanding Denise when she told him
Rue du Mont Thabor, but eventually he shouted
joyfully *oui, oui, oui, oui,* he understood perfectly,
Mont-mumble, mumble, and he turned his ancient
cab with a wild jerk which sent all the girls tumbling
into each other's laps.

"He must be another Frenchman who doesn't understand French," said Fay as they sorted themselves out.

"Not at all," said Denise with dignity. "He's just a
wee bit deaf, that's all."

It was a very enjoyable taxi-ride—well worth the
money, they all agreed, even Julie—and a very good
way to see the sights. Denise pointed out every land-
mark that she recognised and Ricky pointed out a few
more. The only thing was, the ride seemed to go on
for a very long time.

"Surely we must be nearly there by this time?" said
Julie, peering out anxiously at totally unfamiliar
surroundings. "We crossed the river ages ago and the
Rue de Rivoli is only a step from the river—"

"Och, taxi-drivers always take the longest way
round," said Ricky easily, "everybody knows *that.*"

"Yes, but not such a long way round as *this,*" objected Julie.

"Uphill too," said Fay. "*I* don't remember any hills
near our hotel. Denise, are you sure you gave him the
right address?"

"Well you heard me," said Denise, "you heard me
tell him Rue du Mont Thabor—" but she was pretty
anxious herself by this time.

The taxi groaned and wheezed its way upwards, twisted and turned round some very twisting and turning little streets, then drew up. The ancient driver shouted at them, "*Voila, mesdemoiselles*, Montmartre!"

The girls all began to speak at once.

"*What* did he say?" said Ricky in a high squeak.

"Montmartre? Did he say Montmartre?"

"But Montmartre is *miles* away—"

"You ass, you told him Montmartre, not Mont Thabor—"

"I *didn't*! I told you he was deaf—"

"It's the way you keep rolling your *r*'s—"

"Montmartre!" cried Julie. "The fare! Get out quick!"

The girls tumbled out and Julie, glaring at Denise, said *Combien* and very reluctantly handed over the vast amount asked. The ancient man said *au revoir* and ground off in his ancient taxi. There was rather a hostile silence and the trio glowered at Denise.

"You're supposed to be able to speak French," said Julie at last coldly. "That's why we brought you—"

"Could I help it if the man was deaf?" said Denise. "I shouted Rue du Mont Thabor at him about six times—"

"Och well," said Ricky pacifically, "seeing we are here we might as well have a look round—oh goodness, *look*, look up that wee street, there's a bit of that famous church, the Sacré Coeur! Fancy! Let's go and have a look at that—"

They wound their way round some little streets and found themselves in front of the strange white church, more like an eastern palace than a church, at the top of a vast flight of steps with all Paris, it seemed, stretched out before them. They tried to identify famous buildings and did manage to spot Notre-Dame and the Eiffel Tower.

"Goodness, it was worth it, coming away up here, for the view alone," said Ricky.

"Yes," said Julie, "the view *is* jolly nice, but I suppose you realise that we're just about as far from the hotel as we were before, only in the opposite direction? We had better get moving—"

"Let's find one of those pavement cafés and have a drink first," said Fay, "I'm dying, and Ellie kept telling us to—"

If Julie had any objections to this plan she did not have a chance to voice them. Everybody was dying of thirst and they went wandering round the side of the Sacré Coeur again, along the little streets, in search or a café.

Suddenly they turned a corner into a little square; there were ancient little old houses round it and old shops; at least two artists had set up easels and were painting away; and in the middle of the square were trees and coloured umbrellas and under the trees and umbrellas, tables and chairs were set out invitingly.

"That's a bit of luck," said Fay. "Come on, I'm dying of thirst—"

But Ricky had stopped stock-still and was gazing

around her. "But I've seen this place before!" she said in a wondering voice.

"In your dreams, I suppose," said Julie, bumping into her. "Do get on, Rick—"

"But I *have*," said Ricky. "That wee corner and that place called Chez La Mère Geneviève, it's a restaurant, I see, and—goodness, it's the place in my picture!"

She quickly unrolled her coloured print and held it open, and sure enough it depicted the little square in which they were standing. Ricky was much struck by this coincidence.

"It is, it's the same! And look, there's the name of the square written up, the Place du Tertre, I *told* you—"

"So you did," said Fay, "and it's most interesting, but honestly, if I stand here in the sun another minute I'll melt and dissolve into a dew, let's have a cold *drink*."

Unfortunately the tables under the trees were all occupied, and so were the tables on the pavement belonging to the Mère Geneviève, but as by now the girls were desperate, they went into the little restaurant.

It was charming. There were flowers in the windows and blue cloths on the tables and brightly polished bits of old copper on the walls and a great many pictures—mostly of the Place du Tertre and different views of the Sacré Coeur.

They all had *citron pressé*, recommended and ordered by Denise without any misunderstandings. This turned out to be fresh lemon to which they added sugar and water themselves; it was absolutely delicious and they immediately ordered another round. When the waiter brought the second lot of drinks, he put the saucers from under the glasses in a little pile.

"What's that for?" asked Julie.

"Oh, the French waiters often do that," said Denise. "It's so that they won't forget how many drinks you've had. Look, the price is marked on the saucer, and then when you've finished the waiter just counts up the saucers."

So, of course, just for the fun of it, for the fun of seeing a tottering pile of twelve saucers, the girls immediately ordered another round of *citron pressé*.

"Now it's enough," said Julie, counting up the price on the saucers. "Now we had better be going. Don't forget that we have to get back to the hotel and we don't even know the way—"

She scratched in the purse which contained the combined wealth of the trio. "I haven't got enough money left in the kitty," she said. "All those taxis. Give me some money, Fay—"

Fay looked in her purse and handed over fifty centimes. "That's all I've got," she said. "I bought Mitzi's dish and that hankie, remember—"

"Fork out," said Julie. "Denise, Ricky—"

Ricky gave one of her shrieks. "*I* haven't any more money with me! I bought my wee picture—"

"Denise?" said Julie.

"I didn't even bring a purse," said Denise. "I thought that we were only going for a walk—"

"Well!" said Julie. "I think you've all got a jolly good cheek, taking taxis you couldn't afford! Come on, joke's over, fork out—"

They all assured her earnestly that it was no joke, that they really hadn't any money. They practically turned their purses inside out.

"Wait!" cried Ricky. "I've found something!"

This, however, unfortunately proved to be a Scottish threepenny bit that had worked its way behind the lining of Ricky's purse.

"You are a hopeless lot—" Julie began. "You—"

"What about you?" Fay interrupted. "You're supposed to be the treasurer. You shouldn't," she added severely, "have *allowed* us to have all those drinks when we hadn't the money to pay for them."

"Yes, well, never mind that now," said Julie. "The thing is, what are we going to do?" And she eyed the pile of saucers morosely.

The others weren't exactly bursting with good ideas. At least, they had ideas, but not very good ones.

"Well," said Denise reluctantly, "there's my watch. We could hand that over in payment. We should even get some change—"

"Enough for a taxi home?" said Fay hopefully.

"Could we wash the dishes?" asked Ricky. "People in books are always washing the dishes to pay the bill—"

"Or," said Denise, who was fond of her watch, "better still, we could just sort of lend them my watch and come to-morrow with the money—"

"We could knock over that pile of wee saucers," suggested Fay, "and kick some of them under the table—"

These schemes did not appeal to Julie in the least.

"Oh don't be so dotty!" she said in an exasperated voice. "Sell Denise's watch! Wash dishes! Kick the saucers under the table!"

"Well," said Denise rather huffily, for it had been no small sacrifice to offer up her watch, "you think of something better—"

"I have," said Julie annoyingly. "We tell the land-lady what has happened, borrow some money and come back to-morrow and pay. She looks nice, I'm sure she will—" and she nodded across the little room to where a dark, pleasant-looking young woman was sitting behind a sort of counter.

Ricky said in an interested voice, "In what language are you going to ask for this loan?"

"English of course," said Julie firmly. "Denise would probably end up with a dozen snails in a paper bag instead of a loan."

"I would not!" said Denise.

"Yes, well, we can't risk it," said Julie. "Here goes—"

Except for the girls, the restaurant was empty, the morning drinkers of coffee and refreshing drinks having gone and the luncheon customers having not yet arrived. Julie took a deep breath, got up and walked across to the pleasant-faced woman.

She had just opened her mouth and said, "Er—

excuse me, Madame, but—" when a door behind the counter burst open and a young man bounded in. He was wearing a very old, dirty and paint-stained smock and he was carrying a picture held out at arm's length. He said something in French. The pleasant-faced girl's expression became slightly less pleasant and she snapped something back.

The young man's face fell. Then he caught sight of Julie standing hesitantly near the counter and he beamed again. "You want to buy a picture?" he said in English. "Very nice! Look! I am just finished it, the paint he is still wet. You would like to buy it, yes? See, it is nice—" and he turned the picture towards Julie. "You buy, yes?"

"Well, no," said Julie. "On the contrary. The fact of the matter is—"

"Ah, *bon*, nevair mind. Another time perhaps, yes?" interrupted the artist and he bounded across the room and hung the picture on a vacant nail.

Julie glanced at the picture and quickly glanced away again. It was awful, wild whirling blobs of colour that made her head spin.

"Ah, Raoul!" cried the young woman in a voice of sheer exasperation, "*Que tu es bête*! Stop this nonsense with painting and go and cook the dinner! Our custo-mers are arriving at this moment—" The young man bounded off again and she turned to Julie, obvi-ously so cross, that she had to pour out her complaints to someone, even a total stranger, and English at that. "Ah, my husband!" she cried. "Paint! Paint! Paint!

All the day he makes pictures that no one wants to buy! Instead of cooking! Which he can do like an angel! We come to Montmartre from our own village in Bretagne—what do you call it, Brittany, is it?—where he is the best cook in the whole town, and we start our restaurant. But what does he do, does he cook? No, no, no, no, that is too easy. No, he must paint. He has come to Montmartre, the home of so many artists, and he must paint. He *is* an artist, to cook well like Raoul is an art, but no! No, no, no, no, he must paint—" she gave a little rueful laugh. "*Eh bien*, mademoiselle, I must not fatigue you with this *histoire*. You like *l'addition*, the beell, yes?"

This is it, thought Julie. "Well, Madame," she said, "the thing is, we're in a bit of a jam—"

"Jam?" said the young woman. "*Confiture, n'est-ce-pas?*"

"Madame," Julie tried again, "we're in a bit of a mess—"

"Mess?" She thought for a second. "Mess? Meess? English meess?" No, mess defeated her.

"Madame," said Julie bluntly, "we haven't enough money to pay the bill."

Well, once it was all straightened out and Madame understood that the difficulty had nothing really to do with jam, she couldn't have been nicer. She lent them money for a taxi back to the hotel and told them where to find one; she waved aside all apologies; she would have given them luncheon so that they could see for themselves whether Raoul was an artist in cooking, but the girls reluctantly refused, Miss Elliott would be worrying if they failed to arrive back at their hotel.

"*Bon*! It is understood," said Madame. "Another day, perhaps—"

"Oh, goodness, *yes*," said Ricky, the whole party being now collected round the counter, straightening things out. "We'll be back to-morrow with the money."

"Do not give yourselves the trouble," said Madame. "When it is convenient to you and you come again to see the sights of Montmartre—" and amid a chorus of thanks and farewells and *au revoirs*, the girls departed.

"Goodness, I do think the French are nice," said Ricky, as they hurtled down through the streets of Montmartre towards the Rue du Mont Thabor, carefully enunciated to the taxi-driver at least five times. "So kind and trusting."

She changed her tune a little when the taxi-driver, not pleased with his tip, shouted furiously after them as they ran blushing into the hotel. "Well, mebbe they're not *all* kind," she said as the driver's furious yells made the girls wince painfully. "But at least Madame Raoul up at Montmartre is—"

CHAPTER EIGHT

"Well," said Miss Elliott, "we had better keep off taxis for a bit. Living beyond your means, you luxurious girls. We're going to a restaurant near the Etoile for lunch—come along, we'll take a bus."

At the bus-stop Miss Elliott surprised everyone by pulling out a bundle of tickets from a little machine beside the bus-stop and handing them round.

"What's this for, Miss Elliott?" asked Ricky. "Are these our bus-tickets?"

"No, these are tickets to let you get on to the bus," said Miss Elliott. "French people don't like queues much, they think this is fairer. When the bus comes, the conductor will shout out the numbers that he can take. It will be very good for your French."

Of course, Ricky began to dither and began practising her number in an anxious undertone. "*Soizante-douze. Soizante-douze.*" she muttered and worried so much about whether she would hear the conductor when he shouted or would understand him if she did hear, that everyone was on the bus and the chain put across the platform by the conductor before she had realised what was going on.

106

"Hey!" she shouted, beginning to run after the bus. "Hey! You can't do that!"

Various members of the school tour stood on the platform at the back of the bus and waved at her encouragingly, but a lot of good that was, Ricky thought disgustedly. It would have been more to the point if they had stopped the bus. And now the whole terrifying scramble had to be gone through again, she thought, it was awful. The only comforting thing about this situation that she had got herself into, was that now there wasn't a soul to be seen at the bus-stop except herself—surely that meant she was first in the queue? The minute the bus arrived, however, milling crowds simply popped up from nowhere, and before Ricky had time to remember her number and stake her claim, the chain was put up and *that* bus was full and moving off.

Oh *help*, this is too awful, Ricky thought, and had a frightful vision of herself stuck there at that bus-stop for ever, getting old and doddering and dying of hunger but never getting on to a bus.

When the next bus arrived, Ricky's number did not seem to come into it at all, so when the bus filled up and sailed off, she very boldly threw away her ticket and took a new one. Now, she thought, I'm all right, and she feverishly mumbled her number to herself: but when this bus arrived, it was already very full and there was only one place. But that was all right, Ricky thought, this time I really am first and she was just about to put a triumphant foot on the step when again from nowhere appeared an oldish man who did not even have a ticket but who by some very unfair means was allowed on the bus while Ricky was again left standing on the pavement.

A woman at the bus-stop, seeing Ricky's fury and indignation, very kindly tried to explain the reason for this dastardly treatment, but as she explained in French and as Ricky was by this time quite incapable of understanding the simplest word in French, even *oui* or *non* being now beyond her, no progress was made. She briefly smiled her thanks at the woman and marched off. They could keep their buses, she thought furiously, she was going to *walk*.

Miss Elliott had instructed them all carefully, that if they should become separated they must make for the Georges V Métro station in the Champs Elysées, so Ricky went stumping furiously along the Rue de Rivoli towards the Place de la Concorde and the Champs Elysées. She could not get lost, that was certain, the Champs Elysées was unmistakable; the only thing was, she thought, when she came to the corner, could she ever get across that wide and terrifying sea of traffic to reach it?

She stood and thought about it for a minute, and as she was thinking, her glance fell on a flower-seller who was sitting at the corner surrounded by her roses and violets and bright carnations. Violets, Ricky thought. A peace-offering. That's not a bad idea, because by this time I must be madly late and Ellie will be in a temper and Dusty will be in a panic. She glanced at the price of the violets, multiplied by two, started all over again because she had forgotten about francs and was trying to do the sum in shillings and pence, then had a look, in her purse and decided that she could manage it—she was not running any risks *this* time, she had no intention of finding herself stranded in Paris without any money for the second time in a day. But she had a wad of notes in her purse—not a very thick wad actually, but enough, she felt sure, to risk buying two wee bunches of violets.

So she bought her violets and stood at the edge of the pavement, sniffing them and thinking about her plunge into the fierce surge of the traffic; and although she was quite unaware of it, she looked very pretty standing there, with her fair shining hair and her cool cotton frock, sniffing at her violets.

Suddenly, as though he had popped up from the infernal regions like the demon king in the pantomime, a young man stood before her. It seemed to Ricky that he looked furtively to left and right and muttered something, the only word of which that she heard being *printemps* and she wouldn't like to be too sure about that, her French being what it was. However, she answered politely, "*Ah, oui, printemps,*" although as a matter of fact she couldn't think what *printemps* had to do with anything, for as far as she knew *printemps* meant spring and here they were at the beginning of July. However, "*Ah, oui, printemps,*" she muttered politely and the strange young man thrust a small box into her hands and was gone in a flash.

Well, for goodness sake, thought Ricky, what next? She glanced down at the box, a rather grand job in blue plush, and opened it. Inside was a string of pearls.

Ricky nearly fell off the pavement under the nearest bus in her surprise. She looked round quickly, saw the young man disappearing down a stair leading to the Métro, and went roaring after him. "Hey!" she called. "Hey! Stop! You've made a mistake! Stop!"

She clattered down the stairs, saw the dark head of the young man in front of her, ran after him—and had a gate clanged shut in her face by a very surly old lady in a faded green cardigan.

"You can't do that!" Ricky cried indignantly. "Please let me through! There's someone I *must* speak to—"

Understandably enough, the old lady paid no attention whatever to this excited speech, but held out a rather grimy paw.

Oh no, oh no, thought Ricky. If she thinks I'm going to hand the pearls over to her she's very much mistaken! But her brain cleared a second later and she realised that the surly old crone was now opening the gate and apparently all that she wanted from Ricky was her ticket.

Ticket! That was the last thing that Ricky had thought about; but, she thought, seeing that she was in the Métro, she might as well travel by it and get back to the others as quickly as possible to consult them about this strange thing that had happened to her. So she stepped back from the surly old lady to look for a ticket-office.

Having—after a struggle—bought her ticket and having had those awful gates clanged in her face again, although she now realised that it was not spite on the part of the gloomy old crone, but the usual procedure as a train came into the station, Ricky now found herself no better off than before, because she had not the faintest idea in what direction she was going or how to get there. So she was wandering gloomily about and thinking that the Métro might be all very marvellous and everything as people said, but she thought that it was jolly muddling and jolly stuffy, not to say smelly, when lo and behold, she came up against the most splendid map. This map not only showed all the stations but in front of it was also a whole array of buttons. Ricky pressed the one marked Georges V and the map lit up, showing her without the faintest possibility of going wrong which line to take.

Georges V was only three stations away, but by the time that Ricky reached there, she had worked out all about the pearls and why they had been handed to her, and very exciting it was and she was only sorry that she hadn't had a better look at the crook who had done so.

At the Georges V station she found Julie deputised to wait at the meeting-place for her and lead her to the restaurant where, no doubt, the others were already sitting back, bloated with food. Ricky gave one of her shrieks when she saw her friend Julie. "Oh goodness," she said, grabbing her firmly by the arm and determined not to let her go in a hurry, "what a relief to see a kent-face! Thank goodness you waited for me!"

"Well naturally somebody had to wait for you, you daft scone," said Julie, who was a little bit acid owing to the extreme pangs of hunger from which she was suffering. "What happened to *you*?"

"What happened to *me*?" cried Ricky. "Well, just about everything happened to me! To begin with, that frightful bus-stop! I just couldn't even get on to a bus. It was frightful. Every time a bus arrived there was a sort of free fight, everybody yelling and shouting and waving those ghastly little tickets—*they*'re a dead loss if you like, give me a nice, tidy, orderly queue every time—and I simply didn't know what numbers they were shouting! The thing is, these people talk French in a jolly funny way, have you noticed? Not a bit like Ellie and her irregular verbs in the form-room. I mean, you can usually get *some* idea of what Ellie's saying if you really put your mind to it, but there's no understanding these French people at all. And then—" and Ricky became extremely indignant again at the very thought of it,— "and then I really was first in the queue, there wasn't another living soul at the bus-stop, and then what do you think? An ancient sort of old bloke just popped up from nowhere and there was only one seat on the bus and he got it! What d'you think of that for famous French manners? He hadn't even a ticket! He just waved some old card or other and the conductor let him on, and there was I, standing like a spare part, looking silly!"

"So you were silly," said Julie, firmly guiding Ricky to a little street turning off the Champs Elysées. "Ellie told us about that. Wounded soldiers and old people and sick people carry passes and they have special privileges in Paris—reserved places in the buses and tubes and—"

"Oh no!" cried Ricky. "Oh, how awful! Oh, the poor man! Now I feel terrible because I was cross with him and all the time he was a wounded soldier!"

"Och well, cheer up, you didn't know," said Julie soothingly. "So then what did you do?"

"Oh well *then*," said Ricky, cheering up immediately, "then things began to happen! I didn't try to get on to a bus after that, no fear, I just walked. I walked along the Rue de Rivoli and I was just wondering how to get across the Place de la Concorde when I saw a flower-seller, so I thought it would be a good idea to get some violets for old Ellie, you know, to soothe the savage beast, for I knew that by this time she would be as savage as anything because I was going to be jolly late, and I was just standing there, having a sniff at my violets when a man just walked up to me and pushed a string of pearls into my hand."

Julie stopped short and gaped at her.

Ricky nodded. "Yes, it's true! Look!" and she opened the blue velvet box and showed the pearls lying on their bed of satin.

"Well, there's a thing," said Julie.

"I should think so!" said Ricky. "But as I came along in the underground or Métro or whatever they call it, I worked the whole thing out—"

Julie had got her breath back again. "Oh, you did, did you—"

"Yes, and this is how I worked it out—"

"Another crook?"

"Well, yes—but honestly, Button, I can't think of any other explanation. You see—"

"Wait until we've had some lunch then," Julie interrupted. "I'm too weak for one of your crook stories at the moment."

By this time she had guided Ricky along the Rue de Berri, into a doorway and down some stairs into a restaurant. It was big, much bigger than the other little place where they had dined the evening before; there were crowds of people and waiters dashing about, but the school tour had settled themselves nicely at some tables in a little gallery slightly raised from the main part of the restaurant and there were two places being kept for Ricky and Julie at a table with Fay and Ruth and Barbara.

Ricky, flustered and apologetic, nevertheless presented her violets, which certainly seemed to have a softening effect on Miss Elliott and Miss Miller, and slipped into her place at the table.

"I'll tell you, I'll tell you," she said in reply to a shower of questions.

"You bet she will," said Julie, "she has met another crook, so she says. But first of all, could we order our lunch? By this time that repast they call a breakfast isn't even a memory."

So she and Ricky ordered, and, on the others' advice, were just tucking into a vast and varied tray of hors d'œuvres, followed by a most exquisite dish with a name that sounded like *Délice de Sole*, when Ricky took up her tale again.

"I won't tell you about the first bit," she said, "about not being able to get on to that frightful bus, because Button has heard that bit, I'll begin where I'm standing at the edge of the pavement where the Rue de Rivoli joins the Place de la Concorde, and I'm standing there sniffing my violets and thinking—"

"Sniffing violets?" repeated Fay in a tone of mild surprise. She had been too busy eating to notice the presentation of the floral tribute to the two mistresses. "What were you doing that for? Where did the violets come from?"

"I bought them," said Ricky rather impatiently.

"You bought some violets? What was that in aid of?"

"Och, I only bought them to give to Ellie because I thought that by the time I caught up with you again, she'd be hopping mad. Peace-offering, sort of—and I must say," she added, with a reminiscent gleam in her eye, "it seemed to do the trick. Worked like a charm."

"Yes, well, never mind those blessed violets," said Barbara. "Leave out the flowers and get on to the crook."

"But the flowers are important!" said Ricky. "I'm certain that it was on account of the flowers that I got the pearls."

There was silence at the table, except for the cheerful clink of knives and forks, then Fay said plaintively, "I can't follow this story."

"Actually," said Julie, "it's simple. Simple but peculiar. Only Ricky keeps hopping about like a flea. Start again, Ricky, at the beginning. Their wits are slow."

"Well, all right," said Ricky hurriedly before any noisy objections could be raised to this remark. "Well, there I was standing at the edge of the pavement, sniffing my violets when a man came up to me and handed me a string of pearls—"

There was another silence and the girls gaped at her. "Handed you a string of pearls just like that?" asked Fay.

"No, they were in a box—"

"Didn't he say anything?" Fay went on. "Like, *Here are some pearls for you*, or *good-morning* or something. Didn't he even utter?"

"Well, yes, he *did*," Ricky acknowledged, "but you know how impossible it is to make out a word these French people are saying. All that I could make out was the word *printemps*, so I just said, '*ah, oui, prin-*

temps' back in my best French and he handed me the pearls and pushed off."

"Ricky, you're making the whole thing up," said Ruth.

"I am not," said Ricky.

"Show us the pearls then," said Barbara, having now reached a stage in her luncheon where she could bear to put down her knife and fork for a minute.

"Och," said Fay, "Woolworth's, probably—"

Ricky took the blue velvet box out of her bag and opened it. The girls stared in amazement at the pearls, gleaming softly against their satin background.

"Wow!" said Barbara eventually. "They don't look like Woolworth's."

"They look like pearls," said Fay.

"They must be worth thousands!" breathed Ruth.

Julie said, "Let's see them," and held out her hand.

"Well, don't drop them in that fish you're eating," said Ricky anxiously, handing them over. "And don't eat them, either," she added in alarm, when she saw Julie lift the pearls to her mouth and begin to bite them.

"Keep calm," said Julie, "I'm not eating them, I'm testing them. Real pearls feel rough when you bite on them, pearls made of paste are smooth. Or so my mother told me. Interesting, I thought. These are as rough as anything."

"I think it's absolutely mad," said Ruth flatly.

"What's it all about? Why did a total stranger hand you a string of real pearls?"

"Honestly I can't believe they're real," said Fay. "Either Button or Button's mother got it mixed up. I bet it's the real ones that are smooth and the paste ones that are rough."

Julie began to protest indignantly and Ruth said, "Well, I don't see that it matters much whether they're real or not, what on *earth* made this chap hand them to Ricky?"

Ricky quickly retrieved her precious pearls and tenderly replaced them in the box. "I've worked it all out," she said. "It was a mistake."

This did not seem to make the situation any clearer to the girls, so they waited for Ricky to continue.

"This is what I think happened," said Ricky, "I've worked it out. There was this robbery, you see—"

"What robbery?" asked Fay. She was squinting down the menu again, trying to decide on a pudding, and not giving the matter of the pearls her full attention.

"The robbery of the *pearls*," Ricky said. "Maybe just round the corner in the Rue de la Paix—the Rue de la Paix is stuffed full of jewellers' shops, don't you remember, Ellie said so? And the crook," she went on, "was supposed to hand them to an accomplice standing at the corner of the Rue de Rivoli holding a bunch of violets. You see, he gave the password as well— *printemps*, that means *spring* by the way," she kindly added for the benefit of the others,—"and of course

I gave it back, just because I didn't know what else to say. Amazing, isn't it?"

The others agreed that it was amazing, but Julie objected, "Surely even a crook would *know* his accomplice instead of messing about with violets and passwords?"

"Not in a big gang," said Ricky, out of her vast knowledge of the criminal classes. "Often the members of a big gang don't know each other at all."

Julie snorted disbelievingly, and Ricky said, "Well, can you suggest any other explanation?"

Julie unfortunately could not. "What are you going to do now?" she asked. "Go to the police? Tell Ellie?"

Ricky went quite pale at the first suggestion. Go to the police in a strange city and in a foreign language as well? No fear. "Tell Ellie of course," she said, "but not just yet. The papers are bound to be full of this robbery, so I thought I'd wait till there was something said in the papers about these pearls and then I'll hand them over to Ellie—"

"With an air of quiet triumph, I suppose?" Fay murmured.

"Well, naturally," said Ricky good-naturedly. "What's more, I'm hoping for a fat reward."

By this time, Miss Elliott was glancing round the tables to see if her charges were anywhere near finishing their lunch. Most of them had finished, although the thought of touring round the Louvre after what they had managed to stow away was making them rather silent and solemn. Ricky put her pearls away in her bag and hastily shovelled up her last few mouth-fuls of pudding.

"Trailing round the Louvre will be pretty tame after this morning's adventures," she said.

CHAPTER NINE

LIGHT IN THE NIGHT

THE LOUVRE was not exactly tame; it was actually, Ricky said afterwards, jolly interesting in an intellectual sort of way, but very, very tiring on the feet. They saw lots of famous things, such as the Winged Victory of Samothrace and the Venus de Milo of which Julie took rather a poor view as there didn't seem to be enough heads and arms to go round. "One has a head and no arms, and the other hasn't either arms or a head. Still," she added handsomely, "you can see that they're great art because even without heads and things they're still jolly impressive."

Mary Pettigrew was scribbling away in her diary as usual, too busy writing to look properly at the famous paintings that she was writing about. Wendy plodded conscientiously round gallery after gallery; but Ricky, Fay and Julie sat down on every seat that they came to. "I'll look at anything I can see from a seat," Fay said, "otherwise art is out."

"Me too," Julie agreed. "Good old Mona Lisa, you get a dandy view of her from a seat, funny old smug-faced thing that she is—"

As they were now all hot and tired, Miss Elliott had a burst of extravagance and packed them all into a couple of taxis and whipped them back to the hotel in style. They bathed and changed and lay on their beds and rested for an hour, then they set off for Montmartre and the restaurant called Chez la Mère Geneviève.

Everybody liked the little restaurant, and Ricky sat beaming round her happily as if she were personally responsible for the whole place. Madame gave them a great welcome, but Raoul was nowhere to be seen. Ricky hoped that he was in the kitchen, doing his duty for once, and she looked round the crowded walls again with interest, hastily averting her eyes from the blobs and whirls of colour that she had seen Raoul hang that morning. Suddenly, in a dark corner, her eye caught sight of a new picture, half-hidden behind the massive forms of a comfortable middle-aged couple and their three sturdy daughters. Ricky poked Julie with her elbow.

"See that picture?" she said.

"What picture?" said Julie. "There are about five million—"

"The new one," said Ricky, "in the corner, behind the fat old papa with the bald head. Does it remind you of anything?"

Julie looked at the picture, her view rather impeded by the bald head. "'Mm, it does seem sort of vaguely familiar," she said. "Is that the Sacré Coeur? We're always seeing pictures of the Sacré Coeur. I expect it reminds us of one of them. Maybe in the Louvre?"

"I expect so," said Ricky, but she spoke doubtfully.

However as a delicious plateful of food fantastically called *oiseaux-sans-têtes* was at that moment placed before her, she forgot about the picture and turned her full attention to the food.

"*Oiseaux sans têtes* means birds without heads," said Denise helpfully.

Wendy gave an affected little squeal. "Oh, Denise, what a *horrid* idea. Fancy eating poor wee birds without heads!"

"Would you rather eat them *with* their heads?" Ricky inquired with genuine interest and Wendy squealed again.

"I'd rather not eat wee birds at all," she said.

"Och, go on with you, Wendy," said Julie, "they're not birds, they're beef olives, only a jolly, lot nicer than the beef olives we get at home."

Everybody agreed that the meal, if not exactly a picture, was certainly a poem; and when Ricky told them the story of Raoul's devotion to paint in neglect of his cooking, they were shocked. "Anyone can paint," said Barbara, "but I bet hardly anyone can cook like that—"

After dinner, all debts having been paid and compliments bandied to and fro, they said good-bye to Madame and wandered out into the Place du Tertre which was cool and fresh under the stars after the heat of the day; they strolled about and wound their way through narrow little old streets to the Sacré Coeur and looked out at the lights of Paris stretching away below them; until at last they reluctantly dragged themselves away, climbed down the enormous flight of steps below this strange church and took the Métro back to their hotel.

"French food and French beds," murmured Fay, in bed and half-asleep before the others had even begun to undress. "Those are the things I like best about France."

In the middle of the night, Julie woke suddenly. She did not know what had disturbed her—was it a noise, or someone moving about in the room or some sound from Ruth or Barbara next door? She felt about on the bedside table beside her for the torch that she was never without, especially when travelling in these queer foreign places. She shone the beam cautiously round the room; and when it came to rest on Ricky's bed, she paused. The bed was empty.

Now what was old Rick up to, she wondered. Looking for drinks of water, perhaps, and tying herself up in other people's stockings again—she had never known anyone like old Rick for wanting drinks of water—but there was no sound from the bathroom and when Julie shone her torch towards the door, there was no sign of anyone looking for drinks of water.

Julie frowned to herself in the darkness. Rather queer, she thought. Where could Ricky be? As she lay and wondered, she became increasingly uneasy. Supposing that Ricky had heard some noise in the hotel, and had gone to investigate? She had crooks on the brain; if she had heard even a mouse going about its own affairs, she would have assumed at once that it was a crook burgling away, that was certain, but surely she wouldn't have gone to investigate? Ricky wasn't exactly a *brave* sort of person; she would dither so much before daring to venture forth into a dark and strange hotel, that any reasonable burglar would be off with the swag long before Ricky had got herself keyed up for action. Julie relaxed and lay back on her pillows more comfortably—Ricky would never have set off on a burglar-hunt.

But if not prowling around the hotel after an imaginary burglar, then where was she—? Julie sat up again.

Perhaps she had felt ill. That French food was jolly delicious, but it was very rich, with lots of butter and cream and wine in it, and Ricky had eaten plenty of it—perhaps she had felt ill and had gone to ask Ellie for some remedies—Julie lay back on her pillows again.

She lay for about five minutes, which seemed, as a matter of fact, more like five hours, then she sat up again and looked at her watch. It was three o'clock, and she must by this time, she thought, have been awake for about ten minutes or even a quarter of an hour—time enough for Ricky to have fetched twenty remedies for a sore tummy—where on earth *was* she?

Julie reluctantly got out of bed and put on her dressing-gown. Wherever old Ricky was, she had better find her.

She crept cautiously along the corridor. She cast a

rather longing glance towards the lift, but unless she wanted to make a noise like ten thousand tin cans going down the chute and waken the whole hotel, she had better have nothing to do with that ancient and temperamental contraption. She crept quietly down to the next floor.

Here all was silent; so Ricky had not gone to Ellie for medicine or anything of that sort. Julie crept on. She was not particularly given to nerves, but there was something weird and eerie about this cautious prowl through the sleeping hotel. There were unexplained rustlings, and the stairs creaked alarmingly, and every moment Julie expected an irate guest to poke his head out of a bedroom door, demanding to know who was disturbing his night's rest and threatening to call the manager. And, of course, all this time there was no sign of Ricky. It was all most odd.

By the time that she reached the ground floor she was heartily sick of Ricky and all her nonsense: when she turned to her right at the bottom of the stairs into the tiny lounge and saw Ricky standing with her back turned towards Julie calmly reading the paper, she could have cracked her.

"Hands up!" she hissed in a sinister whisper, just for spite.

She should have known better. Ricky gave a wild yell, dropped the newspaper and her torch and tried to hide behind one of the rather spindly gold chairs.

Julie shone her torch on her, for the light from the front hall scarcely reached the dim little lounge.

"Och, get up, Ricky," she whispered impatiently. "It's me."

"Who's *me*?" Ricky whispered cautiously.

"Well, Julie, of course," whispered Julie.

"Oh, help," said Ricky, crawling out from behind her frail shelter, "I thought you were a crook. A crook with a gun. I thought you were going to shoot me. Or knock me over the head."

"I wish I'd thought of it," said Julie. "What are you *doing*? Have you gone out of your mind? You crawl down here in the middle of the night, frightening the life out of everybody, and when I come after you—at great inconvenience, let me tell you—I find you reading the paper. And a French paper at that. If you understood one word in seven, I'll—I'll—*eat* the blessed paper."

"I understood this," said Ricky gloomily. "Wait till I show you."

She picked up the newspaper, which was very conveniently attached to a stick by which it could be hung up and propped it up on a reading-stand. She turned over a couple of pages and pointed. "Look!" she said.

Julie obediently looked. Not that it helped a great deal, although she naturally recognised several words; she didn't spend *all* her time in Ellie's class thinking of other things. For instance, there was the word PRINTEMPS in huge letters—

"What's the French for *pearl*?" Ricky was demanding in a furious undertone.

Julie thought for a moment. Then she said, "Same word, *perle*. Only spelt differently."

"I thought so," said Ricky in a voice of intense disgust. "D'you know what I think this page is? An advertisement for cultured pearls. Being sold at some shop or other called *Printemps*. And in some cases," she added bitterly, "being given away. It wasn't a crook I got mixed up with, it was an advertising stunt!"

CHAPTER TEN

CROOK IN THE KITCHEN

"CRAWLING downstairs in the middle of the night just to read the paper!" Julie scolded as they climbed upstairs again.

"Och well," Ricky said, "I forgot to look in the paper for my jewel robbery before I went to bed, and when I got up in the middle of the night to get a drink of water, I remembered. So I thought that I'd just creep downstairs to have a wee look because I knew that the papers would be there, hanging up by their wee sticks. I'd seen them before. But there was absolutely nothing in the paper except headlines about that child who has been kidnapped. Not a word about a jewel robbery. Only that dotty advertisement. I could have howled when I saw that advertisement. Stupid idea, I think, giving away pearls like that."

"Oh, I don't know," said Julie. "Nice to have the pearls."

Ricky, remembering, said accusingly, "*You* said that they were real pearls—"

"Well," said Julie, "cultured pearls are almost real. They're gritty too, if you bite them—"

Ricky growled crossly, but by morning she had more or less recovered from her disappointment—

after all, as Julie said, she had the pearls—and Miss Elliott, when she showed them to her, said that they were a very pretty string indeed and that she was a lucky girl. They could go to *Printemps* one morning, it was one of the big Paris departmental stores; it would be interesting for Ricky to see where her pearls had come from. All this quite cheered Ricky up.

The plans for that morning were to include a visit to Notre-Dame, Sainte-Chapelle, the Ile de la Cité and the Ile Saint-Louis. Would there be time first, Fay asked, to go to a shop in the Rue St. Honoré?

"Yes, I should think so," said Miss Elliott, "it always seems to take half an hour at least to get this tour assembled. But," she added warningly, "if you're late, we won't wait for you—"

"Oh, we won't be *late,*" said Fay, and swept Julie and Ricky off with her to look at some *petit-point* purses and powder boxes that she had noticed in a shop in the Rue St. Honoré.

"Ma likes *petit-point,*" she said as the three girls hurried along. "I'll get her a purse or something before my money gives out if they're not too dear. I—"

She bumped into Ricky, who had stopped short and was standing still and staring. The others stopped too, to see what Ricky was staring at. "Look!" Ricky said. "Something has happened to that art shop! The window is all boarded up! They must have had a burglary!" Her eyes sparkled. Even to be in the vicinity of a burglary was better than nothing. "I wonder what was stolen? I wonder if it was—" She stopped again, and Fay and Julie, turning to look at her, saw that she had gone quite white.

Julie said, "Ricky, what *is* the matter with you? You keep stopping and starting like Macbeth watching all those ghosts—"

"Ghosts?" Ricky said in a high squeak. "It's worse than ghosts! I've just remembered something! That new picture in the Mère Geneviève, I've just remembered where I saw it before! It wasn't in the Louvre, it was here! It's the Utrillo we saw here, the one that I wanted to buy for Ma!"

The others received this startling news in silence, then Julie said, "How could it be? It couldn't be in two places at once."

Ricky said in a small and anxious voice, "Yes, it could. If it had been stolen from one place and put in another."

There was another silence and Fay said, uneasily, "Oh goodness, I *liked* Raoul. And his wife was a honey—"

The three girls huddled unhappily on the pavement staring at the art-dealer's shop and its boarded-up window, until Julie said briskly, "Honestly, you two! We don't even know if the picture has been stolen!"

"It has, it has!" said Ricky. "I can feel it in my bones."

"What you feel in your bones is nobody's business," said Julie. "Let's go in and find out."

But in this instance Ricky's bones were quite right, the little art-dealer confirmed it: the night before last, his shop had been broken into and the Utrillo stolen. He was in a terrible state still: he even seemed quite glad to see the girls and pour out his troubles to them and tell them all that he knew about the robbery.

It was not much; the window had been cut with skill and the picture removed.

"But Monsieur," Julie said, "the thief won't be able to sell a famous picture like that, will he?"

"Naturally he will be able to sell it," the little man said. "If a collector sees it and wants it, he is not going to ask where it came from, especially if the price is not too high. He will think how ignorant the dealer is, not to know the value of a Utrillo, and how clever he is to get such a bargain. It is probably in some unscrupulous dealer's shop at this moment, waiting for a rich American to see it and buy it."

"Just hanging up there quite openly among a lot of other pictures?" asked Ricky, her face getting longer and longer.

"Perhaps. But perhaps my Utrillo has already left the country—" The poor little man was almost in tears.

Ricky took a deep breath. "Monsieur," she said, "I don't think it has. I think I know where it is—"

She had to repeat this three times before the little man could take in what she was trying to tell him. When he had grasped it, he became very excited. "In Montmartre, you say? Hanging in a restaurant? It arrived there yesterday? *Eh bien*, it is possible—Montmartre is full of rich tourists, looking at the scenes which Utrillo painted, who would buy a Utrillo—you will take me to this restaurant, yes?"

Ricky hadn't quite bargained for this. How terrible to march into that nice wee restaurant with this little art-dealer dancing with rage and denouncing Raoul right and left and tearing the Utrillo off the wall! On the other hand though, she thought, how terrible to steal! She gulped. "Yes," she said, "we'll take you there."

"Then we must wait for a little. Only for a little, until my assistant returns. I want no more robberies, so I will not leave my business unguarded. I will wait for my assistant—he is at the Sûreté, telling those stupid police once more how my Utrillo was stolen."

Feeling extremely uncomfortable, the three girls perched on the edge of three little gilt chairs and waited for the assistant to come and relieve M. Leblanc, which was the art-dealer's name. They wondered uneasily what they had let themselves in for, at least Ricky and Fay wondered and Julie told them. "Now you've done it, Ricky," she scolded in a low voice. "There's going to be a terrible scene at the Mère Geneviève when M. Leblanc arrives—"

"Yes, I know—" said Ricky, gnawing the end of her thumb anxiously.

"It's a terrible thing going into a person's restaurant and accusing that person of stealing a valuable picture. You don't even know if it's the same picture."

"It's the same picture all right," said Ricky gloomily. "I knew the minute I saw it hanging in the restaurant that I'd seen it before, only we'd seen so many pictures that I couldn't just remember where—oh, it's the same picture all right. And you must admit it's queer, that the picture should appear on the wall of the restaurant the minute that it's stolen out of this shop. Raoul can't afford to waste any time, you see—he must sell it before the police get on to him. Och I wish that the assistant would hurry up and *come*, I'm getting the fidgets sitting here—"

The girls did not much care for the assistant when he did come. As a rule the girls liked the manners of the French people whom they met, so different from the dour Scots to whom they were accustomed, but this assistant, according to Ricky, was just too smooth for words. He looked startled when M. Leblanc said that he had a clue to the whereabouts of the Utrillo, but when he heard that it was hanging on the walls of a restaurant in Montmartre he urged M. Leblanc to go and snatch it back with all speed. "Take a taxi," he said.

"Take a taxi," M. Leblanc muttered under his breath as he and the girls hurried out of the shop, "he is so clever at spending my money, that one. If my Utrillo is not recovered, I cannot afford to rush all over Paris in taxis."

However, the thought of rich Americans thronging the restaurant and bidding higher and higher sums for his picture worked on him to such a degree that by the time that they had walked to the Concorde Métro he could stand it no longer and bundled the girls into a taxi. Once more they climbed up to the heights of Montmartre.

The little restaurant looked fresh and delightful in the July sunshine, everything was clean and sparkling, even the double daisies in the window-boxes looked welcoming. M. Leblanc, just for a second forgetting his errand, nodded approvingly. "Charming, charming," he said. "But where is the villain who stole my picture?"

Ricky who, by this time had not the faintest idea what to do and who had even got the length of wishing that she had never begun to interest herself in crooks and the criminal classes, said, "Well, here it is, Monsieur, this is the restaurant—"

M. Leblanc, who seemed to have no doubts as to his course of action, charged straight in, followed by three anxious and rather twittering girls.

One or two people were drinking coffee and sipping *apéritifs* and Madame Raoul was already installed behind her desk although it was early for luncheon. Ricky hurried over to her. "Madame," said Ricky apologetically, "this is M. Leblanc, the famous art-dealer—" She had not the least idea if he was famous or not, but Ricky's geese were usually swans.

She was horrified, however, at Madame's reaction. She went quite white and whispered urgently, "No! No! Don't let him in! Take him away! Take him away immediately!"

So it was true, thought Ricky, and her heart went bumping down to her boots.

M. Leblanc, meanwhile, took one swift look round and went bounding across the little room to the dark corner where the Utrillo was hanging. Ricky, with an anxious smile, more a grimace, really, at Madame, bounded after him.

M. Leblanc took one quick look at the picture then spun round on Ricky with a face of fury.

"Is it it?" Ricky asked, not very clearly.

"That? My Utrillo? Pah!" shouted M. Leblanc.

Oh heavens, oh thank goodness, thought Ricky, now in a sad muddle about what she did want. "Oh, goodness, M. Leblanc, I'm awfully sorry," she said, wondering uneasily if she ought to offer to pay the taxi fare.

Raoul, who seemed to have smelt out the presence of an art-dealer from the seclusion of his kitchen, now appeared at M. Leblanc's elbow.

"You like my Utrillo, no?" he asked.

"No," said M. Leblanc. "I think it is terrible."

Raoul shrugged his shoulders right up to his ears. "The tourists like the copies," he said, "and sometimes even buy one for a few francs. But do not think that I do not agree with you, Monsieur, I prefer the original work. You too prefer the original work—?"

M. Leblanc risked a quick glance at Raoul's original work and shuddered.

"Ah well," said Raoul, making the best of it, "you

will be our guest for luncheon, you and the young ladies who so kindly brought you here—"

M. Leblanc was just gathering himself together for another shudder when Julie managed to mutter, "His cooking is better than his painting—"

"*C'est pas difficile*," M. Leblanc muttered back, but somehow he allowed himself to be led to a delightful table in the window, and they were all seated and M. Leblanc was sipping his *apéritif* and the girls were sipping rather repulsive pink drinks called *sirops*.

Ricky tried again to apologise, but before she had got very far, the most extraordinary little dishes— like the trays my mother bakes little cakes in, Ricky suggested, only so *wee*—were placed before them and M. Leblanc, with a faraway look on his face, was waving them all to silence and sampling the little objects dripping in sauce which he was fishing out of the tiny receptacles with a fork.

The girls sampled too. "Not *bad*," Ricky whispered to Julie. "Nothing to write home about—" In a moment she changed her mind, because Raoul came over and murmured something about *escargots* to M. Leblanc. Ricky gave one of her shrieks. "*Escargots*! That means snails! Were those *snails* that we ate?" Snails were definitely something to write home about, that was certain.

M. Leblanc was nodding benignly, smacking his lips. "*Pas mal. Pas mal*," he said.

By the time that the meal was finished he was not only smiling, but beaming all over his face, congratulating Raoul, congratulating Madame, congratulating the girls who had introduced him to such a magnificent cook.

"He seems to have forgotten about his Utrillo," Ricky whispered to Fay under cover of all these congratulations.

"Good thing too," Fay whispered back. "I thought he was going to be jolly awkward—"

Far from being awkward, M. Leblanc was now promising to spread the fame of Raoul's cooking far and wide over Paris. "Monsieur," he was saying to Raoul, "you will never make an artist. Take the advice of a friend, forget the painting, concentrate on the cooking—" and Raoul was saying that well, perhaps he would when such an authority as M. Leblanc gave him that advice. "Without doubt," M. Leblanc said, "the name of your restaurant will be in the list of the *Restaurants de Tourisme* with two, maybe even three, stars after it," and Madame Raoul was thankfully pressing the girls' hands in turn while tears stood in her eyes.

"But, Madame," Ricky murmured to her as, somnolent and full of good food, they made languid preparations to leave the restaurant, "why were you so alarmed when we came in and told you that M. Leblanc was an art-dealer?"

"Well!" said Madame. "Imagine for yourself! If Raoul had turned out to be a good painter after all! Imagine the tragedy!"

There seemed to be no question about a taxi for the

return journey, M. Leblanc hailed one without, apparently, a thought, and bowed the girls into it; and all the way back to his shop, he was smiling happily and singing Raoul's praises.

Ricky tried again to apologise for taking him on such a wild-goose chase, but M. Leblanc waved her apologies aside. "I have found another artist," he said, "another genius, although of a different kind. Another Escoffier perhaps. Besides," he added, "my Utrillo was insured."

"Oh," said Ricky, "that's jolly good, of course, but don't give up hope yet! I'm sure that you'll get it back. I wish we could help you—" a doubtful glance flitted momentarily across M. Leblanc's face, but was gone before Ricky could be absolutely sure. "For instance," she said, "for instance, you don't think it was your assistant who stole your picture? He looked quite green when you told him that you had a clue to the picture's whereabouts, but he cheered up like anything when you told him that the clue was at Montmartre—"

M. Leblanc looked startled. "*Tiens*!" he said, gazing at Ricky. "Is it possible?"

"Oh help, Ricky," muttered Julie, "now what have you started?"

M. Leblanc wanted to take the girls right to their hotel, but they declined and got out instead in the Rue St. Honoré, at M. Leblanc's shop, and walked along the Rue du Mont Thabor, past the back door of one of the most famous hotels in Paris on their way to their own more modest quarters. And it is a positive fact, that until that moment, they had completely forgotten that they were supposed to be back at the hotel at half-past ten to join the party going to Notre-Dame, and it was now two o'clock.

CHAPTER ELEVEN

THE CROOK IN ROOM FORTY-SIX

Ricky sat on the edge of her bed in her room looking glum. In the words of one of Fay's understatements, Miss Elliott had been a wee bit annoyed. As a matter of fact, in Ricky's words, she had been flaming mad. She had calmed down a little when they had—more or less—explained what they had been doing, that they had been trying to help M. Leblanc, but even so Miss Elliott had said that the girls might at least have telephoned, and the girls had not liked to confess that in the middle of all the excitement at the Mère Geneviève all thoughts of the school tour had completely slipped their minds. So Miss Elliott had decreed that the girls had to be punished; they could each miss an excursion, she decided—and Ricky could start by missing the trip up the Seine by *bateau mouche* planned for that afternoon.

"Couldn't we all miss it?" asked Fay. "A lovely excursion like that, that would be a real punishment—"

Miss Elliott however, was a great deal more wily than even Fay. "Leaving you three together would be scarcely a punishment," she said. "You would be finding lost masterpieces in the hotel dustbins in no time. You can all have your punishments separately."

So Ricky was sitting rather glumly on the edge of her bed. She could have enjoyed going on the Seine, round the Ile de la Cité, on which Notre-Dame was built, and the Ile Saint-Louis, in one of those little white boats. They had seen them waiting at the Pont de Solférino the day that they had been wandering along the quays of the Left Bank. Still, she was so glad that Raoul had not, in fact, stolen M. Leblanc's masterpiece and so glad that he was going to give up painting and go back to his cooking that she did not regret her present punishment. Anyway, she had plenty to do—postcards to write for one thing and her notes to write up, she hadn't done that since the expedition to Schynige Platte. She hoped that she would remember what had happened in between— not that she kept a proper diary like Mary Pettigrew and wrote stupid screeds, all that she did was jot down little remarks like *Explored Montmartre. Dinner at the Mère Geneviève. Gorgeous food.* One entry in fact for July the third, when they were still in Switzerland, con- sisted of *B. in l. C. as c.* This was so cryptic that she had not the faintest idea what it meant; she must remember in future not to rely on initials.

So she pulled her chair up to the table at the window and got busy on her correspondence and her so-called diary and amused herself in between her labours by glancing out of the window at the people in the rooms across the well round which the hotel was built. When enormous clouds came up across the sun and a violent storm broke, she felt that she hadn't missed so much after all, by not going on the excursion that afternoon because the school tour was probably wet to the skin by this time. Besides, it had become so dark that people in their rooms were putting on their lights and she could see them moving about much better.

It was while she was writing and very idly glancing out of the window now and then, that her glances became much less idle and she began to watch the occupants of one of the rooms with close attention. At first there was only a little girl in the room, having her afternoon rest, apparently, but as far as Ricky could make out it wasn't much of a rest, because the child was scattering things, such as books and toys, round her bed wholesale, and was even throwing herself about a good deal and occasionally standing on her head. Ricky found her quite entertaining. But the next part of the programme she only found puzzling; for a woman, quite young and elegant and pretty, came into the room and, as she came in, she locked the door behind her.

That's funny, thought Ricky, locking the door even when she's in the room. You'd think that she was frightened that a chambermaid or someone would come in—

Ricky went back to her postcards, and when next she glanced up the woman was again leaving the room, but as she did so, she carefully locked the door behind her. Ricky was able to see this because the room was next to a landing, and through the window of the landing Ricky could see what was going on outside the door as well as inside, like a stage set. She thought that it was rather peculiar to lock the child in, because she was not a very young child who could come out and do something stupid like falling downstairs. She was at least eight, probably more if she was French and undersized for her age. Ricky got up and leant against the side of the window and watched the child. The acrobatics were beginning again, she was doing hand-springs and standing on her head and she even at-tempted a cart-wheel although that was a bit of a failure because she fell off the bed.

Ricky grinned and the child, picking herself off the floor, glanced up at Ricky's window on the floor above and seeing that she was observed became very self-conscious and dived back into bed and hid under the blankets. She must have found this, however, very boring and stuffy because in a minute or two she came to the surface again and began to perform once more, this time obviously showing off. Ricky could not help laughing because the child was really very funny, and they had got the length of waving to each other when the woman came back.

And the next queer thing happened. For the woman, coming in with a tray on which was a glass of milk and some food, and carefully locking the door behind her once more, looked up and saw the child waving to Ricky. She put down the tray, darted across the room, pulled the shutters close with one hand and adminis-tered what was evidently a hearty slap with the other.

Ricky could hear the child roaring. Odd, thought Ricky. You would think that the mother didn't want the child to be seen.

As the shutters of the child's room were now closed, Ricky went back to her postcards. Her mind, however, was not on them, she could not help wondering about the child. It was almost, she thought, as if the child were being kept hidden away out of sight, most odd…. Eventually Ricky got up and went downstairs to the next floor. She located the landing window quite easily, outside the door of Room Forty-six; but when she looked up at her own window, she could not be quite certain which it was—all the windows looked alike from the floor below. Still wondering about the occupants of Room Forty-six, she went upstairs again, and as she was walking towards her door a gust of wind left over from the tail-end of the storm banged it shut.

Och, footer, thought Ricky, now I'll have to go down to the desk and ask for the master-key.

She did not risk the rickety lift, but ran down the stairs. M. Vernet, who owned the hotel, and who fortunately spoke excellent English, was at the reception desk himself. He handed the master-key to Ricky and grinned at her.

"Mees Elliott told me that you were to be left behind as a punishment," he said.

Ricky grinned back. "Well, I deserved it, you know," she said. "We were expected back in about five minutes and we came back in about five hours."

"*Tiens!*" said M. Vernet, "You were very occupied?"

"Yes, very," said Ricky. "We thought that we were on the track of a very valuable stolen picture, but it turned out to be a wild goose chase."

"A wild goose chase?"

"Yes. I think you call it looking for mid-day at two o'clock."

"*Ah, oui,*" said M. Vernet. "*Chercher midi a quatorze heures.*"

Swinging the key, Ricky turned towards the stairs. "By the way, Monsieur," she said, turning back, "what is the name of the little girl in Room Forty-six?"

M. Vernet bent down to do something behind the desk. When he straightened up, his face was quite red from stooping. "There is no little girl in Room Forty-six, Mademoiselle," he said.

Ricky stared at him for a second, then she turned away. "Oh," she said casually, "I thought there was. I must have been mistaken—"

She strolled off with the key, but as she climbed up to the fifth floor her heart was bumping against her ribs with excitement. Sure as a gun there was something queer about the people in Room Forty-six! And, sure as a gun, M. Vernet knew all about it. She was bitterly disappointed in M. Vernet. She had liked him, he hadn't at all given the impression that he was a crook. But that he was up to something crooked was now obvious—standing there telling fibs and saying that there was no child in Room Forty-six. He must have thought that she was pretty half-witted to be taken in by that story, why he had been red with embarrassment! Obviously he was crooked—the only thing was, she could not for the life of her imagine what he was being crooked *about*.

It was when she was returning the master-key to the desk, having recovered her own and put it in the pocket of her dress, that she had an idea. She was just about to go upstairs again when she caught sight of the newspapers hanging up in a corner of the lounge. She went over and lifted one down and placed it on the stand. It was called *Figaro*, and there on the front page was what she was looking for. The kidnapped child, whom the papers had been full of when Ricky had been searching through them for news of her jewel robbery the night before, was still missing. Her name was Michelle de la Tournay, and her father was a millionaire. She was nine years old and there was a rather smudgy photograph of her. Ricky nearly fainted with excitement: it was the child in Room Forty-six.

She did not know how she was going to wait until the others came in, so that she could pour the news of her discovery into the ears of Fay and Julie. She could not settle to write silly old postcards now that she was in the middle of such excitement. She could not even watch the child in Room Forty-six because the shutters remained obstinately closed.

M. Vernet sent a chambermaid up to her with a cup of chocolate and a *brioche*: an hour, half an hour before she would have been quite overcome by such kindness, now she could only think of it as some sort of sinister bribery. She even wondered if the chocolate was poisoned, but fortunately it wasn't.

The minutes dragged by until the tour came back at five o'clock. They came bursting in, simply full of themselves. They had had a wonderful time, a *bateau mouche* was a delightful way of getting about, they had had wonderful views of Notre-Dame from the river and the Ile Saint-Louis. Of *course* they hadn't got wet, they had gone into the little cabin, when the rain came on and had had *citron pressé*. Poor old Ricky, it was a shame that she had missed it, but Ellie had almost promised that they would go on a *bateau mouche* another day. Had she been terribly bored?

No, Ricky said cautiously, she hadn't been exactly bored, and tried to get Fay and Julie into a corner to tell them her news.

This was not altogether easy. Miss Elliott and Miss Miller, trying to economise, had decided that after the magnificent lunch that they all had—especially Ricky, Fay and Julie, from all accounts—a picnic supper would be perfectly adequate, and they had gone shopping and had brought in fresh rolls and butter and *pâté* and cold ham and cheese and peaches. They would have that, they decided, up in the room shared by Ricky, Julie and Fay because it was the biggest, and then they would go to the Louvre where, on certain Friday evenings, parts of the Louvre were exhibited with wonderful lighting effects. So all the girls kept tramping in and out of Ricky's room, chattering, and Ricky could not get a private word with her friends at all.

Eventually she herded them into the bathroom and locked the door. "You've got to have a bath," she whispered, "because I want to talk to you."

"I don't see the connection," Fay murmured, "but I don't mind having a bath. I'm dying of heat."

So Fay slipped into a tepid bath and lay in it up to her chin, paddling her hands gently while Ricky and Julie sat on the edge and Ricky told her tale.

"There's a most terrible thing going on in Room Forty-six," she began.

Fay slowly shook her head from side to side until her dangling lock of hair was in her eyes. "Oh no," she said, "oh no. Enough is enough. No more of your made-up crooks. You're always promising us crooks and nothing ever comes of it. You get us worked up into a state of terror and excitement and the next thing we know there's nothing to get excited about. Only to-day, this very day, you said that poor Raoul was a crook—"

"Yes, well, I know," Ricky said. "I know I've made a lot of mistakes, but just you listen to this. I'm not making anything up, don't forget, I'm just telling you what happened—"

"All right, then," said Julie, "tell us—"

"Well," said Ricky, "there's a child in Room Forty-six, and M. Vernet says there isn't. She's kept locked up. The woman who is with her—I thought at first that it was her mother but now I'm sure it isn't—locks the door every time that she goes in or out. She's perfectly well, you can see that, she was doing hand-stands and somersaults most of the afternoon, yet she's being kept in bed. My guess about that is that her clothes have been taken away in case she tries to slip out. No one is allowed to see her—her food is carried up to her—and when the woman saw me waving to her, she closed the shutters. What's more, she ill-treats her. She slapped her."

"Oh, pooh," said Julie. "You can't call a *slap* ill-treating her."

"It was quite a slap," said Ricky. "The poor little kid yelled blue murder."

Fay stretched out a toe to the cold tap and turned it on. "Well," she said, "where does the crook come in?"

Ricky said calmly, "The child has been kidnapped. You know that the French papers and bills have been full of this millionaire's daughter who has been kidnapped—"

"No," said Fay, "I don't know. I don't like even reading about kidnapping. It's the most horrible crime. It makes me sick."

"Well anyway, this Michelle de la Tournay—that's her name—has been kidnapped. Age fits and every-thing."

At this point, there was a thunderous knocking on the door and Ruth and Barbara began complaining in loud voices that they were being kept out of the bathroom. Everybody would be coming up for supper in a minute and they hadn't even *washed*, far less changed.

"Okay, okay," shouted Ricky soothingly. "We'll be out in a minute." She began to wash rather sketchily. "Well," she said, "what are we going to do?"

"Oh help," said Fay, "have we got to *do* something again? The last time we did something wasn't all that successful, was it?"

Julie said, "Let's try and skip this visit to the Louvre to-night. Then we can keep our eyes open and see if we can learn anything more—"

Ruth wailed again, "Oh, do hurry *up*, you three—" and the three stopped talking about crooks and hurried up.

CHAPTER TWELVE

THE RESCUE

"Miss Elliott," said Julie after supper, "do you think that Fay and I could stay in to-night instead of going to the Louvre, to get our punishment over? It's awful having it hanging over our heads—"

Miss Elliott privately suspected that it might not be a great hardship for Julie to miss another visit to the Louvre, but she had recovered from her annoyance by this time and felt that she had been a bit hard on those madcaps, making them miss any part of Paris. "Well," she said, "perhaps it would be better. I don't like leaving bits of the party behind all the time."

The picnic supper had been a great success, so much so that some of the girls had rather overdone it, notably Ricky, who was now sitting on her bed looking thoughtful. The others were bustling about getting ready to go out again, and just as Miss Elliott was leaving the room to go and get ready herself, Ricky murmured in a faint voice, "Miss Elliott, I don't think that I ought to go out. I don't feel very well. It would be an awful disgrace to be sick in the Louvre."

Miss Elliott glanced at her sharply. *Now* what scheme had these three in their heads? But Ricky *did* look very pale, and she *had* eaten a great deal, besides she herself was feeling rather more softened towards them, and she did not think that much harm could come to them in the hotel—"I'll bring you up a dose of something to settle your tum," she said, "and then you can go to bed."

"Oh, thank you, Miss Elliott," said Ricky wanly; she hadn't quite bargained for that.

"Anyway, it worked," she said to Julie and Fay when Miss Elliott had gone off to her room to find the medicine. "I never really believed that blotting paper in your shoes would make you faint, but honestly it made me feel jolly ill. And Ellie must have thought I looked ill, to go and get medicine for me."

"Och away," said Julie. "Blotting paper in your shoes! It was all that *pâté* you ate at supper."

Ricky removed the blotting-paper, which she had borrowed from Julie's writing-case—which, of course, had been equipped to the last detail, even including blotting-paper. "Of course, it wasn't the *pâté*," she said, "it was this famous recipe for faintness."

"Well whatever it was," said Julie, "you'd better get into bed. You can always get up again after they've all gone."

Ricky duly got into bed, and duly swallowed the nauseous draught that Miss Elliott brought her. She suspected Ellie of having added a few evil-tasting extras of her own invention, but as she didn't want any fuss and awkward questions, she bravely swallowed it down without a murmur. Then with the usual bustle, banging of doors, rushing from room to room, giggles and muffled shrieks the rest of the party set off, and the three conspirators were left alone.

Keeping an eye on the child in Room Forty-six was all that Julie had bargained for that evening, but Ricky had other plans.

"No, no," she said. "We must rescue her. We might never have such an opportunity again. By to-morrow we might find that she had been taken away to some other hideout. And besides, don't forget that we three might never be left by ourselves again, Ellie's bursting with plans for to-morrow—"

Fay, who was leaning up against the side of the window, idly looking at the shutters that were still folded across the window of Room Forty-six, suddenly straightened up with a jerk. "The woman is going out," she said. "She's locking the door—"

Ricky flung back the bedclothes and was across the room in a bound. "Yes! That's her!" she whispered, as the woman disappeared along the landing in the direction of the stairs. "Now's our chance! Come on—"

"Come on where?" asked Julie.

"Rescue the kid, of course," said Ricky, struggling into her dressing-gown and getting tangled up with the sleeves which were inside out. "Now's our chance!"

"Some chance," murmured Fay. "The door's locked."

"Och I know how to work that," said Ricky. "I did it this afternoon—"

She grabbed the key of the room off the dressing-table and pushed it into the pocket of Fay's dress. "We lock ourselves out and I go down to the desk and borrow the master-key, it's easy. You two go down to Room Forty-six and keep watch—"

"You're not going down to the desk in your dressing-gown!" exclaimed Julie in a scandalised voice.

"Well, goodness, I haven't time to change," said Ricky. "Besides, it'll add veri-veri—whatever that word is, it means it'll make it look more true—"

"Verisimilitude, I suppose you mean," said Fay in a hopeless sort of voice. "I don't see why your being in your dressing-gown will add verisimilitude."

"Oh, do stop arguing," said Ricky impatiently. "Of course it will. People are always getting shut out of their rooms in their dressing-gowns."

Swept along by Ricky's eagerness, Julie and Fay went down to the next floor and stood rather awkwardly outside Room Forty-six. Ricky, risking the rickety lift, descended to the ground floor. She was rather taken aback to find quite a crowd of people, who were milling about the tiny lounge and round the reception desk. However, there was now nothing for it but to sidle up to the desk as unobtrusively as possible.

"Oh, hallo, M. Vernet," she said to the proprietor who was again on duty. "I've done it again, I'm afraid. Shut myself out. May I borrow the key, please?"

M. Vernet, who was trying to attend to six people at once, selling postcards, booking seats for the theatre, telephoning for a taxi and helping two nice old ladies to decide where they would dine that evening, handed over the key with an absent smile. Ricky was delighted to find him so busy. That he was in the conspiracy was certain—otherwise why should he deny that there was a child in Room Forty-six?—so it was a jolly good thing that he was thoroughly occupied with his hotel guests and not likely to come snooping upstairs, spoiling things.

Ricky found the other two lurking uneasily in the corridor outside Room Forty-six.

"Ricky," said Julie firmly the moment that Ricky appeared, "we must have a *plan*. We must—"

"There isn't time," said Ricky, for once not dithering. "We must grab the child and get her upstairs to our room before that woman comes back—"
She bent down towards the door with her key.

"Perhaps the master-key won't fit," said Fay hopefully. "Perhaps there's a different one for each floor."

The master-key, however, fitted all right. Ricky gently pushed open the door and stood on the threshold, while Fay and Julie crowded behind her, looking over her shoulder.

When the little girl saw three strange girls standing at the door she sat up in bed, her dark eyes wide.

"It's all right," said Ricky soothingly. "We've come to rescue you."

This met with no response. The child's eyes became, if anything, bigger, but otherwise she made no sign.

"Oh help," muttered Ricky, "she can't speak English!"

"This is going to test us," said Fay.

She was right. To begin with, nobody knew the French for *rescue*; in fact, Ellie's lessons hadn't in any way prepared them for an emergency like this. They found themselves totally unable to tell the poor child that her troubles were over; that they had come to rescue her. She sat up in bed with her knees drawn up to her chin, solemnly looking at the girls with her big dark eyes.

"You'd think a *millionaire's* daughter would be able to speak English," said Fay in disgust.

Ricky tried a different approach. "*Aimez-vous les bon-bons?*" she said.

"*Oui*," said the child. "*Naturellement.*"

"*Eh bien*," said Ricky laboriously, "*venez. Nous avons*, I mean *nous en avons*—oh help, what's the word for *some*? Och well, never mind, *nous avons des bon-bons en haut*," and she pointed through the window up towards the girls' room.

"*Au ciel?*" asked the child, surprised.

"No, of course not in the sky, you silly little thing," said Ricky, exasperated. That woman would be back any minute, catching them red-handed, while they tried to get some sense into the head of this blessed child. She stopped her more subtle attempts to entice the child and held out her hands. "Come," she said.

To her surprise and dismay the child shrank back. "No, no, no, no," she said in French," my mother said that I must not speak to you girls—"

Ricky wasn't surprised. A kidnapped child couldn't be allowed to talk to a lot of stray girls that she met around the place. "Poor little thing," she said, "that woman has simply terrified her—"

Julie walked across to the bed and lifted the child up in her arms. The little girl immediately began to kick and struggle and even got in some shrewd blows with her fists.

"Come and—help—" panted Julie. "Rescue her first—and explain later—"

"She doesn't look as if she wanted to be rescued," murmured Fay, but she obligingly went to Julie's assistance, and between the three of them they managed to carry the little girl upstairs. She fought every inch of the way.

"Good thing—she isn't—screaming as well—" panted Ricky.

"Maybe she hasn't—thought of it—" panted Fay.

"I don't know—why not," panted Julie, wiping the blood from her scratched face. "She has thought—of everything else—"

However, they reached their room at last and put the child on Ricky's bed and stood back regarding her, panting and—more or less—licking their wounds.

She stared back at them, a hostile expression in her black eyes. "*Et les bon-bons?*" she asked. "*Où sont les bon-bons?*"

"Oh, heavens, yes, the sweeties," said Ricky, and scrabbling in her drawer eventually produced a rather tired bar of chocolate. The child did not seem unduly impressed, which, really, on the whole, thought Ricky, wasn't surprising, but she ate the chocolate.

"What's the next move, Ricky?" asked Fay. The child couldn't be removed too quickly as far as she was concerned.

"Oh help, I don't know—perhaps—well—" Ricky began to dither.

"Obviously we must tell her parents," said Julie briskly. "Er—was there any mention of rewards?"

"Heavens, *I* don't know," said Ricky. "Just getting her back to her mother will be reward enough."

"Oh, sure," said Julie. "You can't help wondering, that's all—"

At that moment, the telephone rang. The three conspirators jumped nervously, and signalled to each other to answer. Eventually Ricky picked up the telephone.

There is no knowing whom she was expecting to hear at the other end of the line, the chief of police himself from her expression, but it turned out to be the reception desk. Would Mademoiselle kindly return the master-key that she had borrowed?

"Help, yes, I will, right away," said Ricky, and shouting instructions over her shoulder to the other two about looking after the child and not letting her put chocolate on the sheets because she was on Ricky's bed, Ricky hurried from the room.

"Where's *she* going?" asked Fay.

"I haven't a clue," said Julie. "But I hope she remembers that she's only in her pyjamas and dressing-gown."

Ricky did not remember a thing about what she was wearing until she was at the reception desk, where the amused glances of the couple who had also shut themselves out of their room and were waiting for the key reminded her that she wasn't really dressed for appearing in public. So blushing hotly, she put the key on the desk and turned away with all speed. Besides, she didn't want to exchange even one word with M. Vernet whom she now regarded as a monster of villainy who was probably thinking at that very moment of the huge ransom sum which would soon be coming his way. So Ricky turned away quickly, but as she made to go upstairs again, she caught sight of the evening papers hanging as usual in the corner of the lounge.

She would have a look at those, she thought. Monsieur de la Tournay's address and even a telephone number might be in the paper; it would be easier to bundle the child into a taxi and take her home than to try to contact the police who weren't likely to believe a word of what the girls had to tell them anyway. So, unconscious once more of her unconventional attire, she hurried across the lounge, took down *Paris-Soir* and put it on the reading stand.

The kidnapping business was on the front page as usual, but reading what was written there, Ricky's blue eyes widened and her heart missed a beat. MICHELLE FOUND said the headlines in huge letters, but in French, of course.

Well, heavens, thought Ricky, that was quick! Fancy having the news in the papers before we've even told anyone!

As she read on, however, she realised that that was rather a silly thought. Michelle de la Tournay, she read, had been restored, unhurt, to her parents that afternoon at three o'clock, after payment of an enormous ransom had been made.

This news made Ricky very thoughtful indeed. If Michelle de la Tournay had been restored to her family at three o'clock that afternoon who, in the name of wonder, was the child in Room Forty-six?

She looked again at the paper. Of course, she knew French wasn't really her best subject by any manner of means... could she possibly have got hold of the wrong end of the stick?

She darted back to the reception desk. M. Vernet, who was busy at the desk, did not now seem nearly such a double-dyed villain. "Er"—she coughed. M. Vernet looked up. "Er—could you please tell me what this means?"

M. Vernet, after years of running a hotel, was well-used to the eccentricities of foreign visitors. He obligingly abandoned his desk and went with Ricky across the lounge to the newspaper stand. But, much to Ricky's consternation, even M. Vernet, whose French must be all right, anyone would think, even M. Vernet was quite clear about the meaning of the headlines and the newspaper report.

"Yes," he said, "it is wonderful, is it not? The child has been safely restored to her parents. It is good, isn't it? To kidnap a child, what a dreadful thing! Kidnapping, it is the worst crime of all—"

C.T.   F

Ricky was feeling so sick that she could not speak, but she nodded dumbly. If you kidnapped someone by mistake, she wondered, would that still count as a horrible crime?

She gulped her thank you's to M. Vernet as best she could, then she tore upstairs. If only they could get the child back before her mother returned!

She arrived at her room quite out of breath. Here she found that the little girl had apparently quite recovered from her fright and justifiable annoyance and was entertaining Fay and Julie to an acrobatic exhibition. Julie had produced the remains of the picnic supper and in between hand-stands the child was managing to tuck away quite a stack of peaches, rolls and pâté.

Ricky stood at the door, panting and gulping. "We must ..." she croaked eventually when she could get enough breath back to speak, "we must ... get her back ... AT ONCE! ... She's the ... wrong child!"

Fay and Julie gaped at her.

"Who's the wrong child?" asked Fay.

"She is," said Ricky, nodding at the little girl. "I—er—I made a wee mistake. She's not Michelle de la Tournay after all."

"How do you know?" asked Fay. "You can't chop and change like that. First of all you said she was Michelle de la Tournay, now you say she isn't. Make up your mind—"

"She isn't," said Ricky in a small voice.

"Yes, but how d'you know?" Fay asked again patiently.

"Yes," said Julie, "how *do* you know?"

"It's in the paper," said Ricky. "Michelle de la Tournay was given back to her parents at three o'clock this afternoon."

"Then who's this wee smout?" asked Fay, jerking her head towards the little girl, who was watching them with bright, dark, inquisitive eyes.

"I don't know," said Ricky. "But we've kidnapped her. And we'd better get her back. Before her mother comes in."

"Oh, *help*," said Julie, "we'd better. Come on then, my wee puddock," she said to the child, holding out her hand, "back we go!"

The little girl put her hands behind her back and glared at Julie mutinously. She had not wanted to come, but now that she was here she didn't want to go away again. She was just beginning to enjoy herself.

"Looks like we'll have to carry her again," said Julie.

"Oh, heavens Julie, *no*," said Fay, touching her scratched face tenderly.

"Well, what do you suggest—" Julie was beginning, when at that moment a most dreadful shriek went echoing through the hotel. The girls rushed to the window. It was just as they had feared. The child's mother had returned and was standing at the door of Room Forty-six while shriek after shriek rent the air.

"Come on," said Julie between shrieks, firmly taking the little girl's hand. "Back to Maman—"

Under the soothing influence of M. Vernet, hastily summoned, the chambermaid, the three girls and the sight of her small child, Maman calmed down eventually—more or less. But that she was still in a great state was obvious. So much so that Ricky, justifiably nervous, couldn't help feeling that the child's mother was going to hand them over to the police after all. She kept wringing her hands and pointing to the girls and talk, talk, talking to M. Vernet, thirteen to the dozen. Ricky's head was beginning to spin. She herself just kept on saying that she was terribly sorry, that it was all a mistake, over and over again.

It did not seem to be getting them anywhere. At last, however, the child's mother had to draw breath, and M. Vernet quickly interposed. "Mesdemoiselles," he said to the girls, "indeed I am desolated. It is *la rougeole*, you understand, what you call, I think, the measles. The poor little one is no sooner in the hotel than she has the measles. Madame her mother is dreadfully upset. Their home is in St. Brieuc, in Brittany, so I cannot turn them into the street when the child is so ill. But then also in my hotel are twelve English misses who perhaps have not already had the measles. I cannot send them back to England where, perhaps, they will all get the measles anyway and blame me and my hotel and people will speak badly of my hotel and I am ruined. But Madame and I, we make a plan—the child will not be allowed out of her room even for one minute, Madame will even lock the door all the time in case the little one, who is now better, you understand, and full of liveliness, should slip out. And all her meals, naturally, will be carried to her by Madame her mother. Madame even tries to hide the child in case any of the English misses should see her and speak to her. And when you speak to me to-night, Mademoiselle," he went on, turning to Ricky, "and ask about a child in Room Forty-six, I am upset and I say there is no child there—"

By this time, Fay and Julie were shrieking with laughter, Madame was beginning to smile doubtfully, the little girl was letting off steam as usual by doing a few somersaults on her bed. Ricky was blushing furiously. "M. Vernet," she said, "please tell Madame that I'm terribly, terribly sorry, but you see I was in my room all this afternoon and I saw all this locking of doors and so on, and then you saying that there was no child in Room Forty-six when I'd seen her with my own eyes, and I—I—I—I'm afraid I thought that the little girl had been kidnapped. So we tried to rescue her—"

M. Vernet now began to laugh and explained the joke to Madame. She, obviously, didn't think it was all that funny, but then the English had a peculiar sense of humour, she knew, so she laughed dutifully and apologised again for the measles and bringing the danger of infection to the girls.

"Och, measles, pooh!" said Ricky when M. Vernet

had translated this little speech to them. "We've all had measles, haven't we?"

Fay and Julie hadn't, but they didn't bother to say so, they all just laughed again and said good-night and the girls privately decided to send a box of *bon-bons* to the little girl, who was really rather a poppet when you got to know her.

"We must do something to soothe her feelings," said Ricky, "after what we did to her."

"We're always sending boxes of chocolates to people to soothe their feelings," said Fay. "Nobody thinks of our feelings."

"We're not supposed to have feelings," said Julie. "We're just Ricky's cat's-paws. From now on let's just cut out Ricky's crooks. She even promised us a nice fat reward this time, and what do we get?"

"Measles, I should think," said Fay.

CHAPTER THIRTEEN

CROOK IN THE RAIN

RICKY behaved with great circumspection for the next day or two. She was sick of crooks and all their doings. As a matter of fact, she didn't believe that there were any crooks in Paris. She put crooks right out of her mind and just settled down to enjoy herself in a different way. This really was not so very difficult because, of course, Paris was great fun and Miss Elliott and Miss Miller kept on arranging interesting things for the girls to do, such as going up the Eiffel Tower in a lift and having lunch up there on the second floor, and going up on the roof of Notre-Dame where Fay and Ricky and Julie had a very enthralling time finding likenesses between their various friends and teachers and the gargoyles, which at such close quarters were fascinatingly horrible.

They went to Versailles too, and admired that splendid palace, and had a picnic in the Bois de Boulogne, and the sun shone all the time, and the only thing was, it was so hot that they had to stop at pavement cafés a great deal for cold drinks and ice-cream. The time simply raced by, and soon there was only Tuesday, one more complete day, because they were going home on Wednesday, and although the plane did not leave till six o'clock, still there would be packing to do and other sad and dreary last-day jobs like that.

"Don't let's do anything special to-morrow, Miss Elliott," said Ricky as they were going to bed on Monday, "let's just wander round the shops again and have lunch at the Mère Geneviève and say good-bye to Raoul—"

Wendy pursed her lips disapprovingly. "There are lots of museums that we haven't seen yet, Miss Elliott," she said. "There's the Musée de l'Homme and the Conciergerie and my guide-book says that the Carna-valet Museum shouldn't be missed, it's in the house where Madame de Sévigné used to live—"

Fay and Ricky and Julie, who had no love for museums and who had never heard of Madame de Sévigné, looked doleful, but Miss Elliott, smiling to herself at their glum faces, said, "Well, Wendy, we can always split forces, you know. Miss Miller or I will gladly take you and Mary and anyone else who wants to go to a few museums and the others can have a good old orgy of shopping."

But to the girls' surprise and disgust, they woke next morning to the drip and hiss of rain. Ricky got up and pressed her nose disconsolately against the window pane.

"Ugh," she said. "Just like Glasgow. The rain's fair stotting off the roofs. Now I don't suppose that Ellie will let us wander round the shops. She'll pack us all off to see those boring old museums with Wendy and Mary Pett."

But Miss Elliott said, "You don't have to go any-where that you don't want to, especially on your last day. If you three don't want to go to the Carnavalet, you don't have to. You can wander for hours under the arches of the Rue de Rivoli without getting wet, or you can go to the Louvre—"

"The Louvre *again?*"

"Not the, museum, the department store called the Louvre—"

"Oh, *well*—" Ricky cheered up.

"But we'll all meet at eleven o'clock at Number Ten, Boulevard Montmartre, and I'll show you a museum which I guarantee you will like, and then we can have our farewell lunch at the Mère Geneviève—"

So Wendy and Mary and the others, armed with waterproofs and umbrellas, went grimly off to the Hôtel Carnavalet, and Fay, Ricky and Julie made straight for the Rue de Rivoli where they wandered happily for quite a long time.

There was no convenient Métro for the Boulevard Montmartre and this mysterious museum that Miss Elliott wanted them to see, but she had told them which bus to take, and although Ricky, as she told the others, would never learn to cope with those Paris buses and those ghastly tickets even if she lived in Paris until she was a hundred, there was no chance of their getting lost while Julie was there to look after them.

Well, not lost in a bus, anyway, but when they left the bus the rain was coming down so hard that they put their heads down and made a dash for it without paying much attention to the bus conductor's directions and found themselves in a narrow, quiet little street. They sheltered in a doorway until the rain should go off a little and allow them to reach the museum without being drenched.

Fay squinted up at the tall houses.

"All these French streets have a sort of secret look," she said.

"It's the grey shutters," said Ricky. "And no proper front doors. Just those big doors like this one which lead into a courtyard before you can get to the front door."

Julie said, "I wish that we could get into a better doorway than this. The rain's dripping down my neck—"

She tried the handle of the small door set in the big door, and it turned. She pushed the door open. The girls crowded round the opening and peered in. Quite a big courtyard opened up before them and doorways and stairs disappeared into dark corners. It was still and grey and quiet, only the hiss of the rain disturbed the silence; a geranium in a pot high up on a window-sill was the only splash of colour against grey walls and grey shutters.

Ricky suddenly shivered. "Let's go," she said.

"Are you mad?" said Julie. "There's a nice bit of shelter over there, in that doorway—"

"It's private. We shouldn't, by rights, be here—"

Julie stared at her. "What's the matter with you? No one would mind our sheltering from the rain—"

"We're late for Ellie—"

"We're not, you know," said Fay, looking at her watch. "It's only a quarter to eleven."

Ricky then came out with her real objection. "It's sort of ghostly," she said. "I don't like it. Look—that dark passage leading to nowhere—it gives me the creeps——"

Julie gave a great sigh. "Och, *you* give *me* the creeps. Is it ghosts now? I suppose you feel that you'd like a change after all those bogus crooks? I suppose that after trying to scare the daylights out of us with all those mad crooks, you think you'll start now on ghosts?"

Ricky suddenly giggled. "No, no, of course not," she said. "Only it's—" she glanced round the courtyard and shivered again, "only it's so quiet and deserted and hidden away …. Anything could happen to us here and no one would ever know—"

"What sort of thing?" Fay inquired with interest.

"Anything—nothing—och, I'm just being daft—nothing, of course. If we stand in that doorway over there we'll be quite sheltered from the rain—"

As it happened, they were both sheltered from the rain and at the same time quite hidden from the big door leading out into the street. The rain was coming down, like slate pencils said Fay, but the girls were nicely sheltered in their doorway, and Julie was feeling much better now that the rain was not going down her neck any longer.

"We'll give it another five minutes," Julie said, glancing up at the small patch of grey sky visible far up above the shuttered windows, "and if it's not off we'll just have to make a dash for it. We don't want to be late for Ellie again—"

"I think that the rain's going off a bit," said Ricky. "It's not nearly so heavy. I think it'll be off in a—"

She broke off as the door into the street began to open very slowly and gently and an extraordinary group came in.

First came a young man—at least he looked young, but it was difficult to see because the collar of his raincoat was up round his ears and the brim of his hat was pulled down over his eyes. He glanced over his shoulder at the man who was following him and muttered something in French. The second man muttered back. He was carrying something large and bulky in his arms. It was covered by a coat or a sheet or something like that, but under the sheet limply hung a pair of feet in buckled shoes.

The girls didn't make a sound, but they stared in amazement at these strange men as they went quickly and silently towards the dark passage which Ricky had noticed and shivered at. But as the men were turning into the shadows, a gust of wind caught at the covering and blew it back. A girl's dark head lolled horribly against the man's shoulder, an arm in a full silk sleeve hung down lifelessly, and as the men disappeared into the darkness of the passage beyond the girls caught their breath. A dagger was stuck in the girl's back and a streak of blood ran across her dress.

The footsteps died away, the girls clung to each other in terror. Ricky's teeth began to chatter. At last she stammered out, "We m-m-must g-g-get away. Or else he'll c-c-come back and k-k-kill us too—"

She stumbled across the wet courtyard to the main door, out into the street and the others stumbled after her. Still huddled together with terror they closed the door behind them with trembling hands, but the sight of an old woman plodding along the pavement opposite under a big umbrella calmed them a little—normal things, apparently, still existed in this horrible world into which they had stumbled.

"What are we going to do?" whispered Julie at last.

"Well, run," said Ricky. "What else?"

"But—but—" Julie was still breathless with fright, "but what about that poor girl? Aren't we going to help her?"

"How can we h-h-h-help her?" said Ricky, her teeth beginning to chatter again, "she's—she's—" she couldn't say the terrible word.

"We must, *must* do something," Julie insisted. "We must get the police—get help—" She looked after the old woman with the umbrella and started up the street after her.

"Let's get Ellie," said Fay.

They blundered up and down the street trying to make people understand where they wanted to go, trying to get away from that dreadful doorway, and, of course, their French completely deserting them. But at last they found a pleasant young woman. "*Numero Dix, Boulevard Montmartre*" she said, "the Musée Grévin? *Comment*, round the corner, mesdemoiselles, only two steps—"

They thanked her hurriedly and ran. Miss Elliott and the others were there, waiting for them.

"Oh, there you are at last," Miss Elliott said briskly. "Come along, we've been waiting for you—"

"Oh, Miss Elliott," Ricky gasped, "we've just seen a most dreadful thing—"

"Well, tell me all about it afterwards," said Miss Elliott absently. "We don't want to waste any more time, or we'll be late for Madame Raoul and the Mère Geneviève."

"Miss Elliott—" Ricky began desperately, but Miss Elliott had gone in to pay for the tickets and the girls surged after her, separating her from Ricky, Fay and Julie.

"Honestly!" said Julie crossly. "Mistresses! They don't listen. We want to tell her about a murder and she just charges off to get the tickets—"

"You don't think," said Ricky anxiously, "that we should abandon Ellie and go to the police instead?"

"Well, it's the same old business," said Julie impatiently. "We don't know where to find the police and we wouldn't know what to say to them if we did find them. No, no, Ellie is our only hope. Come on, we *must* get her to listen."

This wasn't easy. The three girls hurried after the rest of the school and found them streaming with a number of other visitors into a part of this strange museum called the Palace of Mirages. Here they found an enormous temple, many-pillared, stretching away in all directions. They all gasped at this vast place, but Wendy, who had been reading her guide-book as usual, said, "It's all done by mirrors you know, there only are about ten pillars, the rest are just reflections in the looking-glasses." As she spoke, the lights went out, there was a sound of bird-song, and then when the lights went on, the girls found themselves in a wonderful forest stretching away as before into the far distance.

"Yes, yes," said Ricky, "it's all very pretty but we want to talk to Ellie—oh, goodness, oh *help*, what's happened to everybody?" Poor Ricky, whose nerves were not in a very good state after all that she had recently been through, yelped and grabbed Julie's arm, for as she looked around her, instead of the accustomed faces of her friends she saw only ghostly faces whose teeth and eyes gleamed with a strange, pale, green light. "Oh *help*," she cried, "what's happened? You can't tell me *this* is all done by mirrors!"

Everybody, however, was laughing and Wendy was explaining that it was all done by phosphorescent light. The scene changed again, this time to a palace in Spain and everybody exclaimed with delight except

Ricky and Fay and Julie who felt that they had been caught up in a nightmare and only longed to leave this queer place and tell Ellie of their terrible experience.

The school left the Palace of Mirages and the girls found themselves amid scenes of great splendour and interest, scenes from the life of Joan of Arc, a small Mozart playing before Louis XV, Louis XIV at the Palace of Versailles, and amid scenes of terror too, scenes of the French Revolution, Marie Antoinette and the poor little Dauphin in prison.

"But," said Ricky, gazing about her in bewilderment, "this is a *waxwork* show!"

"'Course it is," said Wendy, "what did you think it was? It's the Musée Grévin, Ellie told us—"

"Like Madame Tussaud's in London?" said Ricky.

"Something like," said Wendy, "but the historical scenes are famous. That's why Ellie brought us, to help our French history just by looking. Madame Tussaud was French too, did you know that? Swiss, actually. She was put in prison at the time of the Revolution and because she was good at making wax models, the Revolutionaries made her model all her friends after they'd had their heads chopped off by the guillotine. But she managed to get to England later and toured round the country with her exhibition of wax models—"

Ricky had stopped listening. She was too upset. There was this terrible thing that had happened and instead of doing something about it, she and her friends were wandering round, gazing at a waxwork show. She said distractedly, catching at Fay's arm, "We *must* get hold of Ellie!"

But Fay was standing staring at a scene. "Look," she said, and pointed. In the scene a man was carrying the figure of a girl. Her head lolled horribly against the man's shoulder, an arm in a full silk sleeve hung down lifelessly, a dagger was stuck in her back and a streak of blood ran across her dress.

Ricky gasped. "But that's our murder!" she said.

"Yes," said Fay.

"Different man," said Julie. "This one's in fancy dress—"

"But—but—but—I don't under*stand*!" said Ricky. "Didn't we see a murder at all?"

"I don't think so," said Fay, beginning to laugh. "I think we saw a waxwork figure being brought back from the mending!"

"Och," said Ricky, as they wandered on, now able to enjoy the exhibits rather better than before, "I never felt such a fool in my life! Thank *good*ness we didn't get the length of telling Ellie!"

"Or the police," murmured Fay.

Ricky giggled. "You can't blame me this time," she said. "You *both* thought that we'd seen a crook carrying his victim through the rain, admit it!"

Fay said, "What d'you imagine we *did* see?"

"I expect we were at a back entrance to the Museum and saw one of the models being carried in," said Julie, "but I'm not going to find out. I've had enough.

These waxworks are too jolly lifelike if you ask me, making people think they've got mixed up in a murder—"

"Hear, hear," said Ricky, averting her eyes from the ghastly sight of Marat murdered in his bath, while Charlotte Corday looked on in amazement at what she had done. "We were right to be against museums. It was a great pity that we ever allowed Ellie to persuade us to come to this one. You see what museums lead to. Much better to stick to the shops—"

"And the restaurants, of course," said Fay. "Isn't it nearly time for lunch?"

CHAPTER FOURTEEN

TOO MANY CROOKS

HOWEVER, the time for shops and restaurants and even museums was nearly over. The girls had a last walk along the Seine, a last quick dash to the Rue de Rivoli for forgotten presents, a last cold drink sitting at a café in the Champs Elysées, a last breakfast of *croissants* and coffee ("*That's* no loss," said Fay), a last luncheon and a last delicious helping of *Délice de Sole*, and then they were climbing into the airport bus at the Gare des Invalides and being driven for the last time through the streets of Paris to Le Bourget.

They craned their necks for a last glimpse of the Eiffel Tower and then they sat back in their seats sunk in gloom now that their holiday was really over.

In the aeroplane, however, they cheered up again. It was almost impossible, Ricky said, to be gloomy on an air-trip, because there was never a dull moment. If it wasn't barley sugar being handed round, it was delicious dinner, all neatly arranged on those nice little trays, and then before, almost, they had dealt with that, the fabulous sight of the lights of London spread below them like a fairy carpet.

On the journey, besides the food and the barley sugar and the lights of London, Fay and Ricky and

179

Julie had had the company of a little old lady to en-
liven them. They felt rather sorry for her. Her name,
she told them, was Miss Page, and she was a governess
with a family in Paris. She obviously wasn't a seasoned
traveller like themselves, but fussed a great deal with
her hand luggage, taking things out of her bag and
putting them back again.

When they reached London Airport, she was still
fussing. She grabbed Ricky by the arm as she passed.

"Oh, my dear," she said, "do help me! I have been
re-arranging my luggage and I have taken everything
out so that I can put all my little presents together—
to declare them, you know, at the Customs—and now
I cannot get everything back! *Have* you a spare corner
for my sponge-bag?"

"Och yes, sure," said Ricky without thinking, and
she took the big, old-fashioned, black-and-white
checked spongebag that Miss Page handed to her.

Julie and Fay found her with her case on a bench and
her knee on her case. She was red in the face and
panting. "Oh, there you are," she said.

"Well, of course we're here," said Julie. "Where did
you expect us to be? Up the Eiffel Tower?"

"Oh, funny," panted Ricky. Do sit on this case for
me. I can't get it shut—"

"Why have you got it open?" asked Julie.

"Well, it's that Miss Page," said Ricky, jumping
unsuccessfully on her case.

"Where, in the case?" Fay asked.

"Oh, you're so funny," said Ricky. "She re-packed

her case in order to get all the stuff together that she was going to declare and then she couldn't get everything in. So I've got her sponge-bag. But the thing is, I can't get it in either. You know all those things I collected, presents for everybody and such-like—"

"Let me do it," said Julie, and in her capable way deftly rearranged this and that and in no time had Ricky's things smoothed down and the lid closed.

"Oh, *thanks*," said Ricky and the girls grabbed their bags and hurried along to the counter where the rest of the school tour were waiting with their luggage to have it examined by Customs.

As they passed, they heard Miss Page laying off. "Oh, just a few little trinkets," she was saying, "presents for my nieces you know, a tiny brooch and a handkerchief with the Eiffel Tower embroidered in one corner and an ash-tray for my brother-in-law, he is a *very* heavy smoker, *that* I thought was very original, you see his name is on it—that's his name, William, in my own writing, they did it at the shop while I waited…. Oh, *no*, nothing like that…. Yes, I have lots more to declare, I brought a scarf for my sister, yes, views of Paris, in pink and grey, pretty, I thought, and … Oh, *no*, none of those dreadful things on your list, alcohol and drugs and things like that, and I have no camera or binoculars and as for watches, well, I only have my dear old watch, it was a present from my father on my twenty-first birthday, and *that* wasn't yesterday, young man, but as you see, an excellent time-keeper still, and never loses a minute—"

The girls smiled to each other and the Customs official, looking dazed, as well he might under this spate of words, muttered something. Miss Page's voice rose indignantly, "Well, yes, if you say so, certainly I'll come with you and be examined more carefully, but I tell you this, I think that you are exceeding your authority, young man—" and agitatedly collecting her scattered belongings, she followed the young man through a door behind the counter.

"Och, it's a shame!" said Ricky. "Poor old Miss Page! Where's she being taken?"

The Customs officer looking after the girls' luggage was a very friendly type. He glanced over his shoulder at his colleague and Miss Page disappearing through the door behind the counter. "Just a routine examination," he said unconvincingly.

"Well, I think it's a jolly shame," said Ricky. "Poor old thing, you can see that she's not used to travelling. Jolly shame, I call it—" She went muttering on in this strain until Miss Miller, overhearing, requested her to mind her own business and show the Customs officer whatever she had to declare.

The girls were very soon through Customs and not a penny duty to pay, as they said delightedly. Miss Elliott bustled them towards the airport bus.

"But Miss Elliott," said Ricky, "I can't go yet, I'm afraid. I've got something belonging to Miss Page,

you know, the old lady we travelled with, It's her
sponge-bag, as a matter of fact—"

"Oh, Ricky, no, have you?" said Miss Elliott. "Well,
can't you give it to her?"

"Well, not very well," said Ricky. "She has disappeared somewhere,"

"Then I suppose that we must wait," said Miss
Elliott with a small sigh, and the party watched bus
after bus fill up with returning holiday-makers and
depart for the air terminal in London.

As the time passed and there was still no sign of
Miss Page, Miss Elliott said at last, "Look, this is
ridiculous. Everyone is getting so bored. Miss Miller,
will you go on to the hotel with the others and I'll
wait with Ricky, silly girl that she is—"

"Well, I'm terribly sorry, Miss Elliott," said Ricky,
"but I never dreamt that she would be as long as
this—"

Julie and Fay both offered to stay behind with Miss
Elliott and Ricky, and the four of them settled down
to wait. After half-an-hour they were still waiting.
Planes flew in from Paris, Rome, Switzerland, the
South of France, and crowds of sunburnt holiday-
makers went through Customs, but there was still no
sign of Miss Page.

"This is ri*dic*ulous," said Miss Elliott. "They must be
pulling the poor woman apart—"

They were all by this time excessively bored and
restless and Ricky had even given up trying to apologise
for all the trouble she had caused them by her absent-

minded good-nature. Another half-hour dragged by, and, at last, when they had decided that they might as well give up the struggle and look for a bed for the night, Miss Page appeared, her case, hastily re-packed, bulging, her clothes dishevelled and her hat on the back of her head. "—quite obviously mistaken me for someone else, young man, but I shall accept your apology," she was calling over her shoulder in dignified tones as she came.

Her face lit up when she saw Ricky and she came hurrying over. "So kind!" she said. "So kind! I was quite sure that you would have grown tired of waiting and gone—"

"Och, Miss Page, we wouldn't do that," said Ricky, "we were so *sorry*—"

"Thank you my dear," said Miss Page. "I had a dreadful time, and I intend writing to my M.P. about it—a delightful man, I've written to him several times —do you know"—and she glanced round and lowered her voice—"do you know that they even looked in my pot of *cold cream*! They stuck my nail-file in it and stirred it round!"

"Good heavens, Miss Page!" said Ricky, amazed. "What were they looking for?"

"My dear, I have no idea! But I shall certainly ask my M.P. to find out! Oh, is that my old sponge-bag? Thank you *so* much … So kind…. It is not often that one finds such kindness and consideration in the younger generation these days. It is because you are Scotch, I'm sure. My grandfather was Scotch and I always find myself very much in sympathy with the Scotch—"

"Oh crumbs," Fay muttered under her breath, "are we going to get her family tree now? I want to go—"

But Miss Page, still thanking and explaining and promising to write to her M.P., was gone. They watched her climb into the bus, and their Customs officer, coming out of an office behind the counters at that moment, watched her too.

"Hallo," he said to the girls, "you still here?"

"Oh *yes*," said Ricky, "but that poor old thing, what *did* you do to her?"

"Who, her?" asked the Customs officer, jerking his head towards the bus which was driving off. "I shouldn't waste any sympathy on her if I were you. One of the cleverest smugglers operating at the moment. Yes, one of the cleverest, and yet she looks like somebody's old maiden aunt."

There was a horrible silence. Then Ricky croaked at last, "You're joking. You don't mean it—"

"I mean it, all right," said the Customs officer. "Artful as a barrow-load of monkeys. But we didn't find anything this time. We had a tip that she was trying to get something through, but we didn't find a sausage. We tore her apart, every stitch of clothing was examined, we nearly ripped her case to bits, we even gave her cold cream a good stir. She smuggled through a load of commercial diamonds in a cake of soap once. Which reminds me," he said, a considering look coming into his eyes, "I don't remember seeing her sponge-bag—"

Miss Elliott said in a high unnatural voice, "Well, it has been most interesting, officer, thank you so much for telling the girls, and now we must say good-night—"

"Good-night," said the Customs official cheerfully. "Give my love to Bonnie Scotland," and he grinned at them and gave the girls a huge wink.

Ricky was so upset and so weak about the knees that she could hardly drag herself to the bus. In the bus she was inconsolable. "What *have* I done?" she kept saying. "What have I *done*?"

"I don't know what you've done and I didn't know what to do," said Miss Elliott. "That's why I didn't do anything. Even if we'd told the Customs officer I think that it was too late once she was safely through Customs and they had let her go—"

"She may not have been smuggling anything this time," said Julie, but she did not say it very hopefully.

Ricky burst out, "It's the *injustice* I can't bear. All those crooks that we got mixed up with who weren't crooks at all—crooks in Switzerland, crooks in Paris, crooks all over the place! And then, when we come across a *real* crook we don't recognise her—"

"In fact," Fay murmured in a small voice, "we help her."

They were to spend the night at a pleasant small hotel in Kensington, after a very quick taxi-ride round Piccadilly Circus to see the lights of London.

Ricky was still moaning when they went to bed. Disarranging her case as little as possible, she fished out her pyjamas and her toothbrush and toothpaste. "I'll never get over it," she said. "Never." She gloomily began to brush her teeth. "Ow!" she yelled.

Julie glanced across the room to where Ricky was standing at the basin with her hand clapped over her mouth. "What's the matter?" Julie said.

"'oken my 'ooth," mumbled Ricky. She spat something on to the basin. "Blooming great chuckie-stone in my toothpaste—"

Fay poked at the chuckie-stone. "It's green," she said, "to match the toothpaste."

Ricky glanced at it and glanced at the tube of toothpaste in her hand. "This isn't my toothpaste," she said. She rummaged in her sponge-bag and produced another tube of toothpaste, squeezed in the middle and not at the bottom as she always did, and which always infuriated Julie. "Here's my toothpaste. Well," she said, looking at the others, "where did this come from?"

Fay took the strange tube from her and began squeezing it on to the basin. Every now and then large green lumps appeared.

Julie said slowly, "D'you know something? This is Miss Page's toothpaste. I couldn't fit her old sponge-bag into your case, Ricky, so I took out her toothpaste and stuck it down the side. Unless you put it back?"

"Of course I didn't put it back," said Ricky. "I didn't know that you'd taken it out." She hung over the basin gazing at the green lumps. "But then, what are these?"

Fay said in a breathless voice, "I think … could they be … *emeralds*?"

They were emeralds. Amid scenes of wild enthusiasm, Miss Elliott got in touch with London Airport, and London Airport got in touch with Scotland Yard, and an extremely nice inspector came to the hotel and took charge of the emeralds. It was late before it was all over and the girls sank back on their pillows, exhausted. Ricky still had a broad beam on her face, she had had a broad beam on her face ever since she had discovered that she had two tubes of toothpaste in her possession—her own and Miss Page's. "What a finish to our holiday!" she said. "What a holiday! Will you ever forget it, either of you?"

"Never," said Julie feelingly.

Fay as usual was asleep. But she muttered and turned over. "Too many crooks," she muttered.

THE END